DORA

AND

THE LOST CITY

OF GOLD

Library of Congress Control Number: 2019938809
ISBN 978-0-06-294689-8 (trade bdg.) — ISBN 978-0-06-294690-4 (pbk.)

19 20 21 22 23 PC/LSCH 10 9 8 7 6 5 4 3 2 1
Book design by Erica De Chavez
❖
First Edition

DORA
AND
THE LOST CITY
OF GOLD

THE DELUXE JUNIOR NOVEL

Adapted by **STEVE BEHLING**
Based on the series created by **CHRIS GIFFORD,**
VALERIE WALSH & ERIC WEINER
Screenplay by **NICHOLAS STOLLER**

HARPER
An Imprint of HarperCollinsPublishers

PROLOGUE

"C'MON, DORA!" SAID BOOTS,
the talking monkey.

"Dorrra!" cheered Dora, the six-year-old explorer.

Do-do-do-do-do-Dora!

Do-do-do-do-do-Dora!

Do-do-do-do-do-Dora!

Do-do-do-do-do-Dora!

Dora, Dora, Dora the explorer!

Boots, that supercool *exploradora*!

Need your help! Grab your backpacks!

"I'm a talking backpack!" said Backpack, the talking backpack.

"And your map!" Dora called out.

"Here I am!" said the Map, a talking map.

They have adventures! And they sing songs, too!

Let's go!

Jump in!

Vamonos!

You can lead the way!

"Swiper, no swiping! Swiper, no swiping!" said Dora.

"Awwww man!" replied Swiper, a talking fox.

And that's Swiper! He's a fox who likes to take things that don't belong to him!

"Dora, Diego, it's dinnertime!" called Dora's mother, Elena.

Meet Dora's cousin, Diego! They are best friends. They can't wait to have a big adventure!

Who knows how long they had been playing together? Ten minutes? A half hour? A week? All Dora and Diego knew was that they were both six years old, cousins, and best friends, and had a love of the jungle that couldn't be surpassed.

They had set up an elaborate cardboard-box car right outside of Dora's jungle home, when Dora's mother, Elena, called them in for dinner. The kids had been outside playing, while Dora's friend Boots the monkey had watched. Diego had his own companion, a stuffed jaguar toy that "followed" him everywhere.

"But Mami!" Dora protested. "We were about to explore!"

"Please, Tía Elena, can we explore? Pleeeeeease?" whined Diego.

"Nope," Elena said. "You know you can't play in the jungle at night. Besides, Diego has to be up early tomorrow. He's moving to the city, remember?"

"Oh yeah," Dora said wistfully. "I remember."

"Dora, we've talked about dressing up Boots."

The voice belonged to Cole, Dora's father. He pointed at the monkey in the yard, who up until a minute ago had been wearing a pair of boots that Dora liked to put on him. The monkey was now in the process of tearing the boots from his feet. Then he shoved pieces of the torn boots into his mouth.

"He's a wild monkey," Elena said to her daughter. "He's not meant to be in human clothes."

✿ ✿ ✿

That night, Diego and Dora ate dinner with Dora's parents. The big hit of the meal was the plantains.

"*Delicioso!*" the kids said together.

Then Dora turned her head, and looked out into space. Then she said, "Can you say '*delicioso*'? Say '*Delicioso!*'"

It was quite unclear to whom she was speaking. But since we don't want to leave her hanging, please say "*delicioso*" right now.

This is the part where we wait for you to say "*delicioso.*" Thank you.

"Dora, enough playing," Elena said. "Eat."

Dora and Diego laughed and went back to their meals. Cole looked at his daughter, not really sure what had just happened. "She'll grow out of it," he murmured.

While Diego tried to focus on his plantains, he couldn't help but stare at his aunt and uncle's collection. Being archeologists had its perks. They had an amazing assortment of artifacts, all from the Inca period. They fascinated Diego. He pointed to a map on the wall behind the dinner table, labeled *PARAPATA*.

"Tío, what is . . . Parapata?" he asked.

Cole looked at his nephew and smiled. "Parapata is a great Inca legend. An ancient city, now lost to time."

Cole got up from the table, grabbed an old, worn, leather-bound journal, and tossed it onto the table, where it made a loud sound. Diego and Dora eagerly paged through the book, noting all the incredible illustrations of monkey statues, Inca pyramids, warriors wearing gold armor, and more.

"Legend says they built a temple to honor the growing Inca Empire," Elena explained.

"The largest empire the world had ever seen," Dora said.

"Explorers for hundreds of years have searched for it in vain," Elena added.

The kids turned the page in the book, revealing a Spanish explorer, surrounded by what looked like fierce warriors holding spears.

"And, well, ever since we moved here to the jungle, we have been trying to find it, getting ever closer," Elena finished.

"Is there gold there?" Diego asked.

"The stories say more gold than exists anywhere on Earth," Cole replied.

"So when we find it, do we get to keep the gold?" Dora said.

"I want the gold!" Diego whooped.

"It was my idea!" Dora whined.

Elena laughed. "No, no one gets the gold. We want to document Parapata for archeological purposes. Preserve it, protect it, learn from it."

"We're explorers," Cole said. "Not treasure hunters. And when you're an explorer, well, then the discovery of new places is the treasure."

"What?" Dora said.

"I don't get it," Diego declared.

"They're six, Cole," Elena said. "Treasure hunting is bad, exploring is good."

"Oh," said Dora, getting it.

"Okay," Diego agreed.

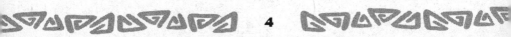

❊ ❊ ❊

Later that night, Dora and Diego were lying in bed, looking up at the stars in Dora's outdoor jungle bedroom.

"I bet the lost city of Parapata has golden statues of jungle cats . . ." Diego said.

"And monkeys! Like Boots!" Dora added with flair. "Monkeys are the best."

"No way!" Diego argued. "Jaguars are way cooler. They run a thousand miles an hour."

"Monkeys can swing and climb and talk to us."

"No, they can't," Diego insisted. "Boots doesn't talk to you! He just listens. 'Cause he has no choice!"

"HE CAN TALK!" Dora hollered.

"I know better!" Diego said. "I'm older than you!"

"By six weeks! I think you're just yelling at me cause you're sad you're leaving!"

"Of course that's why I'm yelling at you!" Diego revealed. "I'm super sad!"

Then it became quiet for a moment, with both kids realizing it was a miracle that Dora's parents hadn't told them to stop talking and get to bed already.

"*Te voy a echar de menos,*" Dora said.

"I'm going to miss you, too, cuz . . . and Boots," Diego said.

Diego said that, of course, because Boots was in bed with them. Like monkeys do.

The three of them closed their eyes, and then they went to sleep under the stars.

❊ ❊ ❊

The next morning, it was time for Diego to leave. Dora couldn't believe it. Not knowing what else to do, Diego produced a candy bar from his pocket, and then broke it in half. He kept one half and gave the other to Dora.

"Until our next adventure, *prima*," he said.

"Until our next adventure, *primo*," Dora replied.

Then Diego got into his parents' car, and they drove off.

Dora stood there, tears filling her eyes as she waved. She ran after the car until it disappeared from sight.

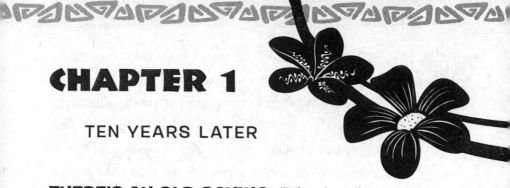

CHAPTER 1

TEN YEARS LATER

THERE'S AN OLD SAYING: "There's nothing like running through the jungle with a GoPro camera on your head while wearing a backpack, chased by a herd of pygmy elephants."

Actually, there's no such saying—that's completely made-up. But still, as far as sayings go, it's very specific.

At any rate, that's exactly where Dora found herself at that moment. Racing for her very life in the dense, verdant jungle from a pack of angry elephants. Yanking the camera from her head, Dora pointed it right at her face.

"Hi, I'm Dora!" she said, not even close to being out of breath. "I'm being chased by a herd of angry pygmy elephants. Can you say 'angry pygmy elephants'?"

Who was she talking to, exactly? That's difficult to say. Impossible, even. There didn't appear to be a single human soul around, aside from Dora herself. Still, if you felt compelled to shout

ANGRY PYGMY ELEPHANTS

now would probably be a good time to do it. I mean, it couldn't hurt, right?

After the whole "angry pygmy elephants" thing, Dora kept on running through the jungle. Now that we think

about it, it's possible that Dora could have been talking to Boots, her constant simian companion. The monkey was perched on Dora's shoulder as the young adventurer grabbed a vine on the go. Her momentum, plus a giant leap, propelled Dora forward, out of reach of the angry pygmy elephants. She took a look below and saw the pachyderms continue to trample the ground in her absence.

When the danger had passed, Dora let loose the vine and slid to the ground. With some red berry juice, she marked the trunk of a large tree with a round *O*. That was her family's symbol—whenever they were out in the wild (which was always), the family would leave the *O* symbol as a way of communicating where they had been and where they were going.

Then it was time for her and Boots to be off once again. They raced toward a river up ahead, and Dora jumped across via a series of rocks. It was a simple hop, skip, and a jump, except that the last "rock" turned out to be the head of a snapping black crocodile.

"Pardon me, black caiman, largest predator in the Amazon!" Dora said, narrating her own adventure, which is a very normal thing to do (don't pretend like you don't do it). Looking down, she was surprised to see a few baby alligators break the water's surface. They snapped their jaws, too. They were cute in the way that things with sharp, pointed teeth that want to eat you are cute. This is to say, not very. Still, Dora couldn't resist.

"Aw, babies!" she said, swooning. Leaving the alligator family behind, Dora continued her trek into the jungle.

"And that's Boots!" she said into the camera. "Hi, Boots!"

Now, Boots wasn't a talking monkey, on account of that's not a thing. So Dora did the next best thing, which was to do Boots's voice for him. "Hi, Dora!" she said, in her Boots voice. "What's today's adventure?"

Here's another old saying we just made up: "The only thing more inquisitive than a monkey is a person pretending to be a monkey." (Pretty good, right?)

Dora then pulled out an old, weather-beaten piece of paper. It was dog-eared, having been marked and remarked so many times. This was her trusty map, and she never went anywhere without it. "Today, we continue our decades-long search for Parapata!" Dora said to her unseen audience via the camera.

As she ran along, Dora passed a tree and notice something bright and yellow. "Oooh, look!" she said, focusing in on the object. "A golden poison frog. Its skin is lethally toxic and can cause full-body paralysis. Can you say 'severe neurotoxicity'?"

Again, unclear who's supposed to say this, exactly. So, if you feel compelled, now's the time to say

SEVERE NEUROTOXICITY

and we'll keep moving.

Dora and Boots proceeded with caution, making sure to avoid even a glancing touch of the frog's poisonous skin. "Bye, deadly frog, have a nice day!" Dora said. The frog just looked at her, because that's something frogs do really, really well.

At that moment, Boots leaped off Dora's shoulder and

took to the trees. Scrambling atop a branch, he nodded his head at something. Dora focused her attention on him and saw what had caught his eye—a gigantic wimba tree that had grown over the entrance to what appeared to be a dark cave.

"Nice catch, Boots!" Dora said excitedly. Then she addressed the camera once more. "Ancient Inca called caves the gateway to the underworld and home to Supay, god of the underworld."

"I've got a bad feeling about this!" said Dora-pretending-to-be-Boots.

"C'mon, Boots!" Dora-as-herself replied. "Let's explore!"

Marking the tree with an *O* in red berry juice, Dora and Boots pressed on. She ran toward the cave, pushing aside the branches of the wimba tree. As she entered the dark entrance, Dora reached inside her backpack and pulled out a small headlamp, which she attached to her headband. With a click, she turned on the light and revealed a swarm of bats flying right out at her!

"Sorry, hairy-legged vampire bat family!" Dora said apologetically. "Didn't mean to disturb you!"

Unnerved, Boots headed straight to Dora and became glued to her side.

"Some say the Inca used caves to hide their greatest treasures from the Spanish *conquistadores*," said Dora, once again talking to the camera. Venturing farther into the cave, she saw some ancient Inca carvings on the cavern walls. Then, seized by the spirit of adventure, Dora started to run. She couldn't wait to discover what was up ahead!

"Whoa!" Dora exclaimed as she stopped short. She felt her foot start to dip, and she pulled back, sending a slurry of pebbles over the edge of a ravine—a ravine she had nearly fallen into! Looking into its inky depths, Dora was silently thankful she hadn't, y'know, gone splat. Then she saw some stone stairs on the other side of the ravine. Above, a shaft of golden sunlight pierced a hole in the cave roof, illuminating a golden monkey statue!

Dora immediately noticed that the monkey seemed to be clutching something in its hands. Was it a map? Dora hoped it was a map. She loved maps.

You probably already figured that out, though.

"C'mon, Boots!" she said, and the monkey, despite probably knowing better, jumped right onto Dora's shoulder. Dora smiled at Boots, determined, and Boots gave her a look that said, *Not only is this a bad idea, but . . . no, it's just a bad idea. Please don't do this. But I know you're going to.* (Looks can say an awful lot.)

"I'm not gonna get into trouble again," Dora said, trying her best to reassure Boots, despite the fact that he didn't speak English. "If you just believe in yourself, anything's possible!"

As if to prove the point, Boots just stared at Dora.

Then Dora was off, sprinting toward the edge of the ravine. As she leaped over the edge, Boots took the opportunity to jump off of his companion's shoulder. Dora sailed out across the void, and . . .

. . . didn't make it!

CHAPTER 2

"I'M OKAY, BOOTS!" DORA said,
as the monkey peered over the edge and into the
ravine, which turned out to be remarkably shallow, which
explains why even though Dora fell, she wasn't injured.

Still, the ravine was just deep enough that Dora couldn't
jump or climb out. "Maybe fetch Mami and Papi?" she suggested to Boots. "And hurry?"

While Boots couldn't understand every word in the English language—a fact we previously established in chapter
one, in case you want to go back and double-check—he was
remarkably adept at picking up on what Dora wanted based
on the sound of her voice, her tone, and recognizing certain
key words, like "Mami" and "Papi"—Dora's parents.

So off Boots went, and Dora was reasonably sure that the
monkey would be back with help. Reasonably.

❈ ❈ ❈

"There," Dora said as she chopped a wooden log into two
pieces. *"Finito."* She placed the two pieces of wood into a
basket and set the axe down on the ground. Then she headed
toward her family's jungle home. Inside, she saw her mother,
Elena, and her father, Cole, as they examined a series of
charts, newspaper clippings, notes, photocopies from old
books and journals, and more.

"Now can I see the statue?" Dora said. Her silent entrance,

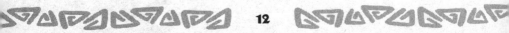

combined with her sudden announcement, caused Cole and Elena to jump.

"Have you chopped all that wood yet?" Cole asked.

"Dora," Elena said, worried and chastising all in the same tone, "if Boots hadn't come and found us . . ."

"I'm sorry," Dora started.

"You're too impulsive, Dora," Cole said, cutting off his daughter. "Exploring is not a game! You're all alone out there, and you don't think about the consequences."

"I know, I know," Dora said, nodding in agreement. "It's just . . ." Then she opened a book from her backpack. "I'm pretty sure it's from the reign of Pachacuti; the markings looked like some sort of . . ."

Both father and daughter looked on, fascinated, as Cole held the monkey statue that they had retrieved from the cave when they rescued Dora from the shallow-yet-not-so-easy-to-escape ravine.

In unison, they said, "Map."

And indeed, that's what the monkey statue held in its grasp.

"Then this is it!" Dora shouted. "The missing piece! And I found it! I found it! We found Parapata!"

Dora couldn't believe her luck. Her eyes went wide, and she looked at her parents as if she had just won the lottery. When she didn't see the same level of enthusiasm, Dora slowed down. "Wait . . . Why aren't you more excited? You already figured it out, didn't you? You know where Parapata is!"

Cole and Elena exchanged a brief look that said, *Yes*, except what came out of their mouths was, "No."

That's when Dora noticed a map on the wall behind them, with a red thumbtack stuck in it.

"You red-tacked it!" she said, pointing right at the tack. "We never use the red tack! You know where it is!"

"Should have waited to red-tack it," Cole said.

"Definitely. That was a bad call," Elena agreed.

"Okay, we figured it out," Cole said, trying to assuage his daughter's feelings. "It's an area of Peru that no one believed the Inca ever reached. But they did. And we're going to prove it!"

Noticing her daughter's hopes going up, up, and up, Elena said, "But you're not going anywhere. You're just not ready. We're responsible for you. Don't you get that? You scared us to death, Dora."

Dora couldn't believe it. All because of that ridiculous ravine thing, she couldn't go? "Mami, I know the jungle!" Dora protested.

"Then why did you end up at the bottom of a ravine?" Elena asked. "Again?"

Ouch.

"Because I'm trying to chart all the local ravines!" Dora answered, and she had to admit, it seemed like a pretty convincing answer.

With a sigh, Elena got up and headed for the kitchen. Then Dora looked at her father, eyes meeting his, giving him the *Please please please you have to do something about this you can't leave me behind* look.

Then Cole sighed and patted Dora's hand. "You do know the jungle, Dora," Cole said. "It's a part of you. So much so

that you don't look before you leap."

"Why's that such a bad thing?" Dora asked.

"Because," her father answered, "we won't always be there to pull you up."

❋ ❋ ❋

"But I don't want to go to the city!" Dora protested. Cole and Elena were busy loading up the family Jeep with Dora's baggage. Which means they were too busy to notice that Dora had emerged from the jungle house carrying her backpack, with a boa constrictor draped around her neck. You know, like you do.

"I won't know anyone there!" Dora continued to whine.

"You'll know your family," Cole said.

"You used to be so close to Diego," Elena added. "I bet he's missed you, too. And your *abuelita* is so excited to make you her famous frijoles!"

Dora rolled her eyes. "You're trying to lure me to the city with beans?"

"You used to love her beans!" Cole offered.

"I found the golden monkey!" Dora said. "Not you! You're both *injustos*. Can you say '*injustos*'?"

(Go ahead, say it—we'll wait.)

"No need for sass, young lady," Elena shot back. "We're going into unexplored parts of the jungle. Militias. Bandits. Tribes who don't like outsiders. Tribes who *eat* outsiders."

Dora shook her head. "That is a false rumor based on Western antinative biases. They don't like outsiders because they take everything they own," Dora corrected.

"She is right about that," Cole said.

"It's not the point," Elena retorted. "Besides, being in the world around kids your own age will help."

"Help what?" Dora asked, genuinely confused.

"Honey, you're wearing a boa around your neck."

"I know," Dora answered. "It's a boa as a boa. It's like a visual pun."

Cole smiled. "It is funny."

"Don't encourage her," Elena said.

"Oh, okay. Put the boa down, young lady," Cole said to his daughter reluctantly. "Take a seat."

Against her better judgment, Dora took the boa from her shoulders and gently put the snake down in the long grass.

"What's happening?" Dora said, looking at her father.

"We gotta have the talk," Cole said.

A horrified look crossed Dora's face. "What?!"

"Not that talk!" Cole quickly clarified. "No, no, no . . ."

"Another talk," Elena interjected. "About the dangers of the big city."

"Right," Cole said, looking relieved. "Okay, look. You may know about the jungle, but you don't know about the big city. But we do. We're hip to it."

"Yeah," Elena said, backing up her husband. "We know things."

"Right. Like, people are going to invite you to dance parties called 'raves,'" Cole said.

"The people there are called 'ravers,'" Elena added.

"They're gonna have glow sticks, candy necklaces, and

hacky sacks. The music will sound like this . . ." Then Cole started to make sounds from his mouth, which Dora guessed was maybe supposed to sound like beat-boxing? Maybe?

"This is not good?" Dora asked.

"No," Elena said. "This is not good. If someone wants to take you to a rave, what do you say?"

"'Yes, thank you'?"

"No!" Cole shouted. "You say 'No!' You shove them to the ground and shout, 'No, I will not go to an illegal rave with you!'"

Dora nodded rapidly. "Um . . . okay?"

Then Cole took his daughter's hand again and pulled her close. He hugged her tightly. "Just be careful out there, *mija*. That's all we're trying to say."

"Here, take this satellite phone," Elena said, handing the device to Dora. "Call us anytime. You can track our coordinates on your map."

"It's not the same," Dora said. "I'm an explorer. Like you."

Elena took Dora by her shoulders. "The whole world is out there for you to explore," she said. "Go see it, make friends. That's real exploring."

Dora looked pensive, unsure. "But . . . I don't know how," she admitted.

"Yes, you do," Elena argued. "Just be yourself, Dora. You survived the jungle. High school will be easy. Now come on, or you'll miss your flight."

Mother hugged daughter, and Elena took a step back.

"No monkeys in the city, honey," she said.

Found out, Dora opened her backpack. Out jumped Boots.

Dora gave the monkey a big hug and wiped a tear from her eye. Then she gave Boots a scratch on his chin, because he really liked chin scratches.

"It'll be okay," she said to Boots. "And I'll be back before you know it. I promise. Hey, look after Mom and Dad for me."

Then Dora climbed into the Jeep along with her parents. As the vehicle pulled away, Dora waved at Boots. The sad monkey waved back.

CHAPTER 3

THE PLANE FLIGHT, AS far as plane flights go, was dull and uneventful. This was a good thing. Exciting and eventful plane flights usually mean something happening, and "something happening" is not exactly what you want to experience when you're on a plane.

So when Dora stepped out into the city airport, she was ready for some excitement. And she got it. For one thing, there were so many people! Dora had spent so much time in the jungle by herself, or with only her mom and dad, that she had almost forgotten what it was like to be around other human beings!

"Hello!" Dora said as she passed by a woman wearing a big yellow hat. She didn't know her, but that didn't stop Dora from saying hello to her.

Or from saying, "Hello!" to a little boy holding a blue balloon in one hand, his father's hand in the other.

Or from saying, "Hello! Hello! Hello!" to literally every single person she passed on her walk through the airport. She didn't even notice the looks that people were giving her. Not annoyed, but just surprised—like they weren't used to this sort of friendliness.

But the excitement of seeing so many people quickly wore off, and soon, Dora found herself feeling hemmed in. There were too many people! As she headed down the escalator, she

was being jostled and elbowed by strangers. Not on purpose, of course. It was just a side effect of being in a big crowd.

Dora was starting to think that she didn't like big crowds.

✾ ✾ ✾

"Do you see her?" Nico asked. "It's been so long. What if we don't recognize her?"

Nico and his wife, Sabrina, stood by the street curb, watching as passengers exited the airport. A teenager wearing sunglasses looked up from his phone, then did a double take.

"I think that won't be a problem," Diego said, looking up as a young woman came sliding down the banister before them. Right as she reached the bottom, she leaped off the banister, then hopped a barricade with no effort, and ran right for Diego.

"Tía Sabrina and Tío Nico!" Dora shouted, happy to see someone she actually knew.

"Dora!" they hollered. "Welcome to the city!"

Dora's aunt and uncle reached out for a hug, enveloping their niece. Diego, on the other hand, stood off to the side, wanting to play it cool.

He should have known that wasn't gonna fly with Dora. His cousin quickly embraced Diego, hugging him so tight that his spine definitely cracked.

"Diego!" Dora exclaimed. "You're so skinny and tall like a palmito tree! You don't even look like you!"

Diego gave Dora a pat on the back. He looked a little at a loss, almost like he was embarrassed to be seen with his

cousin. Then Dora surprised him by returning his pat on the back with one of her own. The pat was a little hard, and by that, we mean that it caused Diego to stumble forward.

"We're gonna have so, so much fun!" Dora shouted.

"You are way more energetic than I remember you," Diego observed.

"And you are trying to grow a mustache but do not have enough hair for it!" Dora said, staring at Diego's upper lip. "There are so many people here! Like too many! But if millions of rain forest ants can live together, I guess, so can we. Let's go!"

❀ ❀ ❀

A while later, Dora and her family pulled up in front of a row of Craftsman-style houses. The warm wood made Dora feel at home, or at least, as at home as she could have felt in the city. They parked in front of Tía Sabrina and Tío Nico's house, and Dora was thrilled to see her sitting on the front porch.

Abuelita Valerie!

Dora flew up the path to the house and embraced her grandmother.

"Abuelita!" Dora said. "I've missed you!"

"Dora!" said Abuelita Valerie. "It's so good to see you, *mijita*! Look at you, such a big girl now! And still with the bangs! Tell me your favorite dishes and I'll make them all."

Not missing a beat, Dora launched into a list of delicacies she had been dreaming about on the plane flight over. "Okay! *Pirarucu de casaca, crema da capuazo, cachama ahumada . . .*"

"Frijoles it is!" replied Abuelita Valerie.

✿✿✿

Dora had to admit that the frijoles were delicious, even though they weren't exactly at the top of her list. Still, there was no way she could say no to her *abuelita*. After dinner, Diego showed Dora the room where she'd be living while she attended high school with him. The room had been decorated just for her! Everything was pink, with tastefully matching pillows, bric-a-brac, and more—it was perfect for a teen girl.

Or so they thought.

"Wow," Dora said, speechless for a moment. "So much pink . . . and everything matches!"

"Yeah," Diego said. "My parents thought you'd like it. So . . . what have you been up to the past ten years?"

Unsure about the matchy-matchy room, Dora plunged ahead nevertheless, and proceeded to unpack. She cleared a shelf full of accessories, making room for a stack of explorer books.

"Last ten years?" Dora finally answered. "Well, you drove off with your parents, then I was kinda sad, then I went inside for dinner, where they made me flan to make me feel better, and I shared it with Boots. He says hi, by the way . . ."

While Dora hit the highlights of the past ten years, she took out two pictures—one of her parents, and the other of Boots.

"Boots?" Diego asked.

"Our friend!" Dora responded. "About yea high? Brown hair? Eats bugs? You know, Boots. A monkey."

Diego looked legit confused. "I had a friend who was a monkey?" he asked.

"*Is* a monkey," Dora corrected. "And yes. You did. You were friends with lots of jungle animals. In fact, you know more about animals than anyone I ever met!"

"Pretty sure you're confusing me with someone else," Diego said.

Dora ignored her cousin's obvious confusion. "Hey, I brought you something."

Then she dug into her backpack and pulled something out, handing it to Diego. It was about an inch across, maybe four inches long, and crusted over white.

"What . . . is . . . that?" Diego asked, suddenly afraid.

"The candy bar you split with me before you left the jungle. Remember? Where's yours?" Dora said.

Diego was grossed out. No one had ever brought him half of a ten-year-old candy bar before.

"Err . . . I don't know," Diego said. "I probably ate it . . . like, ten years ago?"

The news did nothing to slow Dora down. "Oh, okay! I thought we were going to mush them back together. But that's cool. No biggie. This is gonna be great. You and me. A couple of explorers back together again!"

"Right," Diego said, feeling the need to back away slowly, without making any sudden movements. "Okay . . . well, get some sleep. *Buenos noches, prima.*"

Dora looked up at her cousin and smiled. *"Buenos noches, primo."*

Diego exited the room, leaving Dora to her unpacking. She gazed at the candy bar half. Then she shrugged and put it in her mouth.

It wasn't bad, as far as ten-year-old candy bars go.

Ready for bed, she just felt like something was off. Grabbing the comforter, she opened the window to her room and climbed out to sleep in the garden behind the house.

CHAPTER 4

DORA HAD NEVER TAKEN a school
bus before, which meant she had also never walked
to the school bus. So it was already a day of firsts, before she
even arrived for her first day of high school in the city.

As she walked down the street with Diego, Dora found
herself singing:

> "Backpack, backpack
> Backpack, backpack
> On the backpack loaded up
> With things and knickknacks too . . ."

Diego was almost afraid to ask, but he did anyway.
"Um . . . what're you singing?" he asked.

Dora turned to face her cousin. "I always sing," she
answered. "Boots likes it. And it keeps me calm and happy!"

Just then, the bus headed down the street and pulled up in
front of Dora and Diego. He looked at his cousin from head
to toe. "Hold on, do you mind?" he asked.

"Mind what?" Dora responded. In a flash, Diego removed
Dora's headband, then roughed up her hair, untucked her
shirt, and crumpled it a little so it looked wrinkled, kind of
worn. Y'know, cool.

"Is this to fit in with the indigenous people?" Dora asked
curiously.

"If you can bring your overall energy down a little, that would be great," Diego said. "No big deal."

Dora wrinkled her brow. "I feel like you're saying it's *not* a big deal, and yet your face is suggesting it *is* a big deal," she said.

Diego shrugged. "I just want you to have a good first day," he said, turning toward the open bus door. Before he took a step, he looked back at Dora and said, "Oh, and if I don't talk to you, don't take it personally. We're all just trying to survive. High school is a horrible nightmare."

With that, Diego hopped aboard the bus, leaving a confused Dora in his wake.

✽ ✽ ✽

The bus was full of noisy teenagers, everyone talking as loud as they could, or so Dora thought. She was quiet, merely observing, taking in all the details. She noticed that Diego was quiet, too, but then she figured that he was just being "cool," which seemed to be something that occupied a lot of Diego's time.

When the bus arrived at the high school, Dora took a deep breath. "Just be yourself," she whispered. Confidence was never a problem for her, but Dora had to be honest—she was feeling a little out of her depth here.

She jumped off the bus with characteristic energy, right next to Diego. As they entered the school, Dora couldn't help herself. She started to say hello to anyone and everyone!

"Hi!"

"Hi there!"

"Hola!"

"Hiya! I'm Dora!"

We'll spare you the rest of it, but suffice to say, it went on like that for some time. And every time Dora said "hello" or some variation thereof, Diego flinched a little. This was not what looking cool was all about. He hurried into the school, walking slightly ahead of his cousin.

Soon, they were at the entrance, waiting in line to have their backpacks and school bags checked by security. They would have to walk through something Diego called a "metal detector," which was new to Dora.

When it was her turn, Dora went right through the metal detector without any hesitation. You know what also didn't hesitate? The beeping sound coming from the metal detector. It went

BEEP!!!!!!

and it was loud and shrill and annoying.

Dora turned to the security guard as he rummaged through Dora's backpack.

"Hola, I'm Dora!" she said, as the security guard pulled out a small, circular object from her backpack.

"What is this?" the guard asked, eyeing the object with suspicion.

"A flare," Dora answered matter-of-factly. "In case of emergency. It's totally safe."

To show just how safe it was, Dora took the flare, broke it, and offered the bright, burning flare for the guard to see, smoke and all. The guard took a big breath and blew out the

flare. Then he grabbed it back from Dora and put it into a box that was marked *FIRE HAZARD*.

Not done yet, the guard then pulled a small bottle from the backpack.

"Iodine pills," Dora explained. "To sanitize water."

The guard dropped the bottle into another box, confiscating them from Dora. By now, a line of students had begun to form behind Dora, all waiting for their turn to go through the metal detector so they could enter the school. At this rate, they would all be late.

But that had no bearing on the security guard, who kept on removing item after item from Dora's backpack.

"Personal generator."

"Two-way radio."

"Five-day emergency food supply."

"Descending ring."

"Lantern."

"Ice axe."

"Crampons."

"Nitroglycerin for cave-ins."

"OneLink Shelter System with DoubleNest Hammock. You know, for cliff sleeping."

And the list went on, and the guard dumped all of it— ALL OF IT—into a series of boxes. He then handed the backpack to Dora. "Yeah. You can't bring any of this in here," he said, amazed at just how much stuff Dora had managed to cram into her backpack. "Pick it up after school."

Dora was surprised to find the only thing left in her

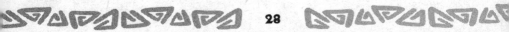

backpack was a yo-yo. "But I can bring my yo-yo?" she asked, incredulous. "You realize a yo-yo is by far my most dangerous weapon?"

Before the security guard could say a word, the school bell rang, and Dora could hear a collective moan from the line of students stuck behind her. They were now all late.

Just like Dora.

Annoyed, Diego grabbed his cousin, and they headed inside the school.

❋ ❋ ❋

"In order to survive here, the most important rule is—"

"Don't jump into murky water because you never know how deep it is?" Dora guessed, cutting off her cousin. They were walking down the hallway. Dora had her notebook open as she hurriedly wrote down some high school survival tips from Diego.

"No," he answered flatly.

"Never forget to finish your course of malaria tablets?" Dora tried again.

"No! You can't get too excited about stuff," Diego said. "Just be chill." The minute the words came out of his mouth, Diego was pretty sure that Dora had no idea what that meant.

As they walked down the hallway, they passed by a kid who was handing out cupcakes. It was Sammy Moore, the class president.

"Cupcakes for charity!" she shouted. "Save the rain forest!"

Dora was immediately in Sammy's face. "What happened

to the rain forest?" she asked, as if there had been a sudden emergency.

"It's being destroyed . . ." Sammy said, not sure of what to make of this new student.

"Oh no!" Dora hollered. "Which one? Daintree? Yasuni? El Yunque? Hoh? Tongass? Kakum?"

Sammy was stumped. She wasn't really sure which one. So to be safe, she said, "All of them. Probably Kakum."

"Ranching and agriculture are the greatest threats facing the Amazon today, but with focused conservation and plant-based diets, I believe the rain forest can thrive again!" Dora said.

Sammy stared at Dora, her eyes narrowing as she looked at the new kid. "Who are you?" she asked. "Why are you smart? And what are you doing in my school?"

It took Dora barely any time to process this, and she immediately said, "Dora. Homeschooled by professors. Parents misjudged me as irresponsible and lacking in socialization."

The words registered with Sammy, who was trying to determine if this new kid was a threat to her. Unsure, she put on her best fake smile and said, "I'm Sammy! Great to have you here, Dora. I've been desperate for efficient subordinates! Have a cupcake on the house!"

Dora took the cupcake, then ran ahead to catch Diego.

"She seems nice," Dora said.

"She's not," Diego said without hesitation. "That's Sammy Moore. Honor roll student, tri-varsity athlete, and class president."

Dora nodded. "So she must be very admired by her peers."

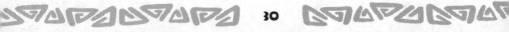

"What?" Diego said in disbelief. "Her? No way! Everyone hates her. She's literally the worst person on Earth."

A few steps later, and the pair had reached Diego's locker. Dora noticed a kid standing next to the locker, wearing headphones, and doing something on his phone. He was also wearing a T-shirt that had a picture of what looked like the universe, along with an arrow pointing to a particular spot with the words, *YOU ARE HERE.*

"Hi, I'm Dora!" she said to the kid. "Cool shirt."

The kid didn't seem to hear her, Dora thought, so she tapped him.

This had the great effect of making him a) jump, and b) scream. His headphones fell off, and he was suddenly face-to-face with Dora.

"We're not there," Dora said, and saw immediately that the kid had no idea what she was talking about. So she pointed to his shirt. "Earth. We're more like over here. Want me to correct it?"

"Uh . . . yeah?" the kid said. Dora thought he seemed a little out of it. No matter. She reached into her backpack and pulled out a marker. Then she drew an arrow to what she thought was the correct place in the universe.

"There we go!" Dora said, proud of her handiwork.

"Are you into astronomy?" the kid asked.

"Of course I am," she answered. "Who isn't?"

Once more the school bell rang, and Dora jumped, looking all around her.

"What's that?" she shouted. "Is there a problem?"

"It's the morning bell," Diego said, grabbing his cousin. "We gotta go!"

As the cousins walked down the hall, Diego said, "That's Randy Waren. You don't want to talk to him, either."

"Why?" Dora asked, genuinely not understanding. The kid seemed really cool, and he was into astronomy!

As if in answer, Dora saw two big students walking down the hall. They passed by Randy, and one of them checked Randy right into his locker with a loud SLAM.

"That's why," Diego replied.

Dora frowned.

"Don't look at me like I'm the jerk," Diego said. "I don't make these rules here. I was just born into this system."

"Okay," said Dora, but it seemed pretty flimsy to her. She watched as her cousin put on his sunglasses, and headed into a classroom. "Why are you wearing sunglasses? It's not sunny indoors!"

Diego didn't say another word. Dora simply continued to take notes in her book and headed inside.

✱ ✱ ✱

"Let's see who did the reading last night," said the English teacher. "Who is Moby Dick, and what's this story trying to teach us?"

Dora was sitting in the back of the class with Randy. She saw Diego sitting up toward the front, right behind Sammy. Sammy, of course, had her hand raised practically before the question had been asked. But Dora knew the answer to the question, so she raised her hand, too.

 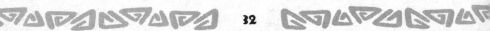

The English teacher smiled, then pointed at Dora. "Oh, thank god, someone else! My prayers have been answered. You're new, yes? Well, say hello!" the teacher said to Dora.

Sammy's eyes bore right into Dora as she spoke. "*Hola*, I'm Dora! I'm Diego's cousin."

Diego covered his face with his hands.

"And Moby Dick's a whale. The novel exemplifies the Western writer's nostalgic appropriation of colonized and indigenous cultures, which explains its reified status in American fiction."

The English teacher stood there staring, clearly impressed. "Where did you transfer from, Dora?" she asked.

"The jungle," Dora said. "My parents are both professors. I do a lot of reading."

Then Dora was rudely interrupted by the sound of another student coughing. Only they weren't exactly *coughs*. What they really did was say, "Dork-a," in a way that sounded like a cough.

The whole class laughed.

Dora wasn't really sure what to feel. But Diego? Yeah, Diego was mortified.

❋ ❋ ❋

Dora looked at herself in the bathroom mirror. With her mussed-up hair, untucked shirt . . . it just didn't look like her.

"Not sure I made myself clear earlier," came a voice from behind. It was Sammy. "Statistically, there are point-eight full-ride scholarships per public school awarded to girls in this state, so if you're gonna take a shot at the queen, you

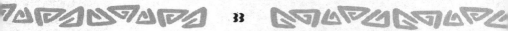

better not miss. There's nothing more dangerous than a wounded animal."

"A lot of things are more dangerous than a wounded animal," Dora argued. "A healthy one, for a start."

"Stop. Just stop," Sammy said, glaring at Dora. "I'm watching you."

Dora watched as Sammy stormed out of the bathroom. She wondered what that was all about. Turning her attention back toward her reflection in the mirror, Dora straightened her hair and put her headband back on. Then she tucked her shirt in.

She smiled at herself and thought, *Better*.

Maybe now that she looked like herself again, things would go more smoothly.

✤✤✤

"Goodbye!"

"Bye!"

"See you!"

"We did it!"

"Finished school!"

"Great job!"

"Home time!"

Just like when she arrived, Dora said something to every single person she passed on the way out of school. She noticed that her cousin was steps ahead of her, and his head was locked in a downward position, like he was surveying the floor for signs of microscopic life.

CHAPTER 5

WHEN THEY REACHED HOME,

Abuelita Valerie was sitting on the front porch.

First to arrive was Diego. Granted, he was always trying to look cool these days, so he didn't often have much of an affect. But she could tell today that something was off, even for him.

"How was school, my little ones?" Abuelita said. Then she took note of Diego's sour expression. "Everything okay?"

Dora came up from behind Diego, a broad smile on her face. "Great!" she said, completely oblivious to Diego's mood. *"Perfecto!"*

"Yeah," Diego said. "Great. Perfect." His tone said the day had been anything but. Turning around, he faced Dora. "Listen. That day cannot happen to me again. Ever. So let me lay down some high school rules for you . . ."

> **ONE:** *KEEP A LOW PROFILE.*
> **TWO:** *NEVER APPEAR ENTHUSIASTIC ABOUT ANYTHING.*
> **THREE:** *WE DON'T KNOW EACH OTHER.*
> **FOUR:** *NO ONE, I REPEAT, NO ONE ACTUALLY DANCES AT A SCHOOL DANCE.*

Dora listened to the rules, and vowed she would do whatever it took to make her cousin happy. Even follow these clearly weird, nonsensical rules.

✻✻✻

As the school days went by, Dora was slowly getting the hang of things. Kind of. She was doing her best to follow Diego's rules, but it was hard. It all went against her nature. Dora was naturally friendly and outgoing, inquisitive, and eager to talk to people about who they are and what they like to do.

This, of course, was the exact opposite of Diego's rules.

Still, Dora tried. Even when she had mac 'n' cheese for the first time in the cafeteria, and she completely freaked out because it was MAC 'N' CHEESE AND IT WAS SUPER DELICIOUS, Dora did her best to keep it together and "be chill." In this case, "be chill" looked an awful lot like running up to each member of the cafeteria staff and shaking their hands and congratulating them on a job well done.

Then there was the time she saw Diego eating lunch with all his friends from the soccer team. She waved at him and started to approach the table. And when she sat down at the table, Diego's friends got up at once and left. At least Randy was sitting there, and he moved down at the table to sit next to Dora, even if he never did lift his eyes up from his phone.

She didn't say much to her parents about it, though. They had such little time to talk on the satellite phone as it was, and Dora didn't want to occupy their time with her struggles at school. Sometimes she would call them just to leave messages, like, "Hey, Mami, Papi, call me when you can. I'm fine. Totally fine! Don't I sound fine? We're going to the Natural History Museum Friday, so fun! Why wouldn't I be fine? Miss you. Miss Boots. Miss . . . everything."

One day, when she was leaving a message like that one on the walk home, she saw a black van on the street behind her. Maybe it was her imagination, but she thought it was following her. But that couldn't be right. She got on the school bus, heading for home, vowing not to give it another thought.

❈ ❈ ❈

December twelfth. The school year had been flying by, even though to Dora, it moved more like a sloth. The winter dance had arrived, and suddenly Diego's advice about no one actually dancing suddenly made sense. Everyone was supposed to come dressed as "your favorite star," like the banner said.

"Everyone."

First off, there was practically nobody in the high school auditorium that night. Dora saw Randy sitting off to the side, glued to his phone as usual. He was wearing a T-shirt with a big letter *H* and a little *1* next to it. Among the kids, Dora could also see Sammy, wearing a judge's robe, her hair pulled back, looking kind of like Supreme Court Justice Ruth Bader Ginsburg.

And then there was Diego, who was hanging out with his soccer-team friends, wearing a Messi Barcelona shirt.

AND THEN there was Dora, who had shown up dressed like an actual star.

The sun.

She went right over to Randy, because she was sure that he would get it.

"You're the sun!" Randy said, confirming that he did indeed "get it."

"You're hydrogen!" Dora shot back, gesturing at the *H* and *1* on his shirt. "It's what all stars are made of. Great job!"

Randy looked like he was about to say something, but nothing really came out. So Dora kept on rolling. "I love this song!" she said, nodding to the music that filled the auditorium. "Randy, you want to dance?"

Randy's face drained of all color. "I can't really dance," he stuttered. "But I can hold my breath for seven minutes. My parents left me unsupervised at the community pool a lot. Pretending to drown was a good way to get attention. The lifeguards gave me juice boxes. Wanna see?"

Without waiting for an answer, Randy took a deep, almost comical breath, and held it. Not knowing what else to do, Dora smiled.

And Randy kept holding his breath.

And holding it.

And holding it.

"Okay, no problemo," Dora said, as it appeared Randy might be going for a new record. "I love dancing. I'm really good at it!"

So she headed out to the dance floor. Dora noticed that literally no one else was dancing, except for one older teacher, who was getting her groove on near the punch bowl.

Technically not on the dance floor, but close enough. But Dora didn't care. She was there to dance!

"What are you doing?" Diego said, interrupting her.

Dora sighed. "I'm done not being into things," she began. "I like dancing. I'm going to dance the dance we used to dance. Remember?"

Diego was frustrated. "For one night, just leave me alone."

Dora shrugged. From the moment she hit the dance floor, she was on fire. "The Elephant!" she called out, then formed one arm into a trunk, putting it up and down as she moved from side to side.

A bunch of kids started to notice, and they nudged each other, laughing in that particularly cruel way that only kids seem to have mastered. They slowly formed a circle around Dora, who continued to dance, even as they clapped sarcastically. Some even had phones out, recording Dora's dance. Then a spotlight shone on her.

"Look," said one of the mean kids. "It's 'Disco Dork-a'!"

This got Sammy's attention, and when she saw what was happening, she said, "Oh my god, she's going to have to transfer schools."

But if any of this registered with Dora, she didn't show it. Instead, she kept on dancing, having the time of her life. She announced, "The Peacock!" next, and fanned her hair behind her like a peacock's crest. Dora scratched at the floor with her feet, wheeled around in a circle, and flapped her hands behind her. Then she circled around her cousin and his friends.

"Come on, *primo*! *Baila!*" she called out. "You know this one!"

The soccer team started to laugh as Diego tried to back away. One of his teammates said, "Yeah, *primo*! Let it all hang out! Show us your jungle moves!"

"Dance, Diego, dance!" the soccer team screamed. "Dance, Diego, dance! Dance, Diego, dance!"

The chanting grew louder and louder, until Diego couldn't stand it anymore. Finally, the music stopped. The kids "applauded" Diego and Dora.

Diego stormed out of the auditorium.

Dora followed.

❊ ❊ ❊

"At least I got people dancing," Dora said, trying to lighten the mood.

"They were mocking you!" Diego said as he wheeled around on his cousin. "Laughing at you! And me! You've been here for weeks. How do you not see that?"

Dora set her jaw. "I see it. I'm not stupid. But I have to be myself. It's all I know how to do!"

"Well, stop doing it!" Diego fired back. "Just for like one day, stop being you and just be normal!"

The words stung like a swarm of bees. "Diego, we used to be so close," Dora said, reaching out to her cousin. "Why are things so different now?"

"Because this isn't the jungle, where you can do whatever you want and have a monkey for a best friend!" he bellowed. "This is high school! This is life or death! And it was hard enough already without having to take care of the class weirdo!"

If the words Diego had uttered earlier stung, what he said in that particular moment was like the bite of fire ants. It hurt.

Dora turned and walked away without saying another word.

CHAPTER 6

SHE THOUGHT SHE MIGHT feel better when she got home, but she was wrong.

Tía Sabrina and Tío Nico's home wasn't really home. It wasn't the jungle.

The jungle was where Dora's parents were. She missed them terribly, especially after her blowup with Diego. When she got to her room, she picked up the satellite phone and tried to call her parents.

The phone rang.

And rang.

And rang.

No one was there.

The phone went to voice mail, and Dora left a simple message: "Mami, Papi, where are you? Please call me."

She hung up, then looked at the phone to check her parents' coordinates. They hadn't changed in the last few days, and she wondered if anything was wrong.

Slumped on the floor of her closet, Dora wrapped her arms around her knees, cradling herself. She felt something she wasn't used to feeling. Defeat.

"Sometimes we all need to hide," came a voice. It was Abuelita Valerie. She came into the room, entered the closet, and sat down on the floor right next to Dora.

"I just want to talk to my parents," she sighed, trying very hard to hold back tears. "But they haven't picked up in days."

"That's why you're upset?" Abuelita asked. "You miss your parents?"

Dora thought about it for a moment, not sure what she should say. "I do, but . . . I guess I never felt lonely when I was alone in the jungle. Now that I'm surrounded by kids, I feel alone all the time."

There were no words that Abuelita could think to say that would comfort Dora in that moment better than a big hug.

"Even Diego hates me," Dora said, snuggling into Abuelita's hug.

"You are *familia*," she said. "He loves you. He's just too worried about being like everyone else. Afraid to be himself. Unlike you. *Tu eres fuerta, mija . . .*"

"Abuelita," Dora said, not sure if she wanted to hear the answer to the question she was about to ask. "Am I a weirdo?"

Abuelita almost chuckled. "No more than the rest of us . . ."

Dora frowned. "That's not a 'no.'"

Then Abuelita Valerie squeezed Dora's shoulder. "Let's get you some frijoles."

CHAPTER 7

DORA WASN'T SURE IF things
were better, worse, or somewhere in between.
They just . . . were. School kept on coming, and she kept
on going, the days running into one another. At last, it was
time to take the field trip to the Natural History Museum,
which was at least one thing that Dora had been looking
forward to.

"Here's the scavenger hunt list," the teacher said, handing
out papers to the assembled students. Dora took hers and
noticed Diego standing nearby. They didn't acknowledge one
another. It had been like that since the night of the dance.

Randy was there, too, taking his paper without his eyes
ever once leaving his phone's screen. Sammy was there as
well, doing her best to pretend to ignore Dora while totally
not ignoring Dora.

"You know the drill," the teacher continued. "First team
to complete it wins. Team up in groups of four and start taking photos! And if anyone needs me, I'll be in the cafeteria,
per usual."

The class immediately formed into groups of four
students, and they raced off to complete the museum
scavenger hunt. Diego went to his soccer-team friends to
try to join a group, but they literally turned their backs on

him. It was a no-go, not after the "Elephant and Peacock" ·
dancing affair.

It wasn't long before Dora realized that she, Diego, Randy,
and Sammy were the only ones left without a group. And
that meant that they *were* the group.

"You've *got* to be kidding me," Sammy said, noticing the
same thing.

"Looks like a great team to me!" Dora said, trying to
sound cheerful.

Randy immediately perked up, and stared into Dora's eyes.
"What about a team?" he said, looking a little infatuated.

Diego, on the other hand, simply groaned and said, "Of
course this is happening."

As the group reluctantly made their way through the
museum, Sammy surprised Dora by coming over to her and
whispering, "There's a real icy thing happening between you
two. What's going on?"

Dora and Diego looked right at one another. Mustering
her courage, Dora said, "Well, I'm glad you brought it up—"

But before she could continue, Sammy cut her off. "I'm
not losing," she said. "I don't do last, so let's get our big-girl
pants on."

Any chance Dora had to address the problem with Diego
had just flown out the window.

Sammy started to read from the scavenger-hunt list. "Find
something that's more than a thousand years old. Oldest relic
gets two extra points."

Diego nodded in the direction of another group of students taking a photo of a nearby plaque. "Those guys just took a photo of that ceramic jug," he said. "It says 300 BC."

"We just have to find something older! Come on!" Sammy announced, her competitive spirit taking charge.

"Could you be any bossier?" Diego asked.

That did it. Sammy whirled around and let Diego have it. "'Bossier'? For real? What's next? 'Shrill'? Or am I being too 'difficult' for you? You left that out of your Misogyny 101 class." Diego just stood there, feeling about two inches tall. Randy looked on as well. "What? What is it? Do you have something to say?"

Randy couldn't even shake his head. "I'm just so scared right now" was all he could manage.

While Sammy laid into Diego, Dora noticed a poster on the wall announcing, *TREASURES OF THE ANCIENT EGYPTIAN WORLD. COMING SOON.*

"What about this Egyptian exhibit?" Dora wondered aloud.

"I think I may be able to help you."

Dora turned around and saw one of the museum guards talking to her. She was older, maybe around the same age as her mom. She looked friendly. "Overheard about your scavenger hunt," the guard said. "You were checking out the Egyptian posters. Smart girl."

"When does it open?" Dora asked excitedly.

"There's the rub," the guard replied. "Two weeks. They're unloading it today in the basement, but that's off-limits to visitors."

Dora sighed. "Anything Ancient Egyptian would be the oldest relic by far," she said out loud.

"Sure would," the guard answered. "Look, I got kids. I get it. If it means that much to you . . . there may be a way for you to get down there somehow." The guard then took her security card and walked over to the door next to the poster. She opened the door and then entered, leaving the door slightly ajar.

Dora smiled.

✤✤✤

Not even a minute had passed before Dora had gathered up the members of her team and dragged them through the supposedly off-limits door. Dora was sure that this was a great idea, maybe even the best, and would guarantee that they win the scavenger hunt.

She was the only one who felt that way.

"This is a bad idea," Diego said as they walked down a basement hallway. There were boxes and crates on either side of them. He followed Dora, who took the lead. Sammy and Randy were right beside him.

"This best not be some wild-goose chase," Sammy said, immediately regretting the choice of words, knowing full well that Dora would now proceed to tell her something about geese.

"Let's hope it is," Dora said. "I love chasing wild geese! Until you catch them. Then it is not fun! A caught goose is just the meanest . . . Either way, you all want to win, right?"

Sammy looked at Dora. "We're not losing. Come on, people!"

The teammates pressed ahead and turned a corner. It was just endless rows of shelves, filled to the top with boxes of varying sizes. Ahead, they could see the loading dock, which trucks used to bring in the exhibits. There, they saw a large wooden crate that looked like it had just been unloaded, with packing material still inside.

Dora headed down an aisle, talking all the while. "It's grouped by origin. The Ancient Egyptian stuff should be down this aisle." She thought that the group was still behind her, not realizing that Diego, Sammy, and Randy had taken a different aisle.

As Dora turned a corner, she bumped right into another guard. "Oh, hi!" she said cheerfully as usual. "I'm Dora. I can totally explain why we're down here."

"Oh no!" Sammy said, peering between boxes on the shelves into the other aisle. "She's been caught! Hide!"

"Where? Where?" Randy said, panicking. Suddenly, a black-booted delivery man walked in, causing Randy, Sammy, and Diego to scatter.

Thinking fast, Diego pointed to the large shipping crate. "There!" he said, and all three dove inside, hiding among the packing materials. The delivery guy just walked on by and didn't seem to notice them.

So they hoped.

From inside the crate, the three tried to see what was

going on. Randy found a small hole in a knot in the wooden wall and peered outward. "I don't get out much," he whispered, "but are delivery guys normally armed?"

✾ ✾ ✾

"Look what I found sneaking around," said the guard, grasping Dora's shirt and marching her toward the "delivery guy."

"Ah, an interloper?" said the delivery guy. "A thief? Or maybe . . . an explorer? *Hola*, Dora." The man took off the hat he had been wearing and set his cold, heartless gaze on Dora.

How does he know my name? Dora thought. But this was no time to be thinking. She looked around for an escape route, and her heart soared when she saw the security guard who had helped her before!

"You gotta help me!" Dora called out. But rather than be comforted, Dora's stomach turned when she saw the security guard's twisted smile.

"I guess we win the scavenger hunt," she said, pushing Dora toward the open crate where Diego, Sammy, and Randy had been hiding. Once she was inside, the delivery guy slammed the crate shut.

"Dora! What's going on?" Diego called out.

"Is this still the scavenger hunt?" Randy asked.

"What?" Dora answered. "What are you guys doing here? Wait, no, let me out! Let me go!"

The delivery guy spoke from outside the crate. "Sleep tight, Dora. When you wake up, you'll help us find your parents, and then . . . Parapata."

Dora gasped and felt her whole body filling with dread. Then she noticed the air seemed a little thin, and she thought she could smell something inside the crate. Was it . . . gas? She didn't have much time to think before she started

to fall

asleep.

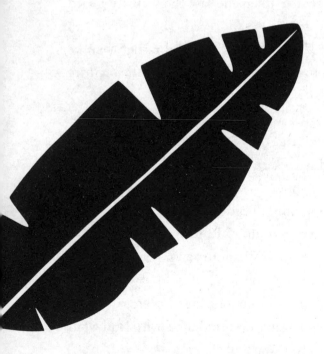

CHAPTER 8

DORA HAD NO IDEA how long she had been out for. Maybe a minute . . . or an hour? A day? As she awoke, she could feel the crate shifting and jostling beneath her. She was lying on the floor of the crate. Rolling over, she saw that Diego, Sammy, and Randy were slowly starting to come around as well.

"What's happening?" Randy asked, his voice groggy. "Where are we?"

Dora sat up enough so she could look through an air hole in the crate. She couldn't believe it. The crate was being unloaded from the back of a cargo plane! As the crate kept on moving, she could see that they were on a runway, out in the jungle. In the distance, she could see a couple of guards . . . yes, it was the "museum guards!" The woman and the man who had grabbed Dora. She could see a large flatbed truck on the tarmac and immediately assumed that the crate would be loaded onto it.

"I think . . . we're being unloaded from a plane," Dora said, her voice still a little shaky from the gas.

Sammy managed to get to her feet and looked out another hole.

"That's not funny, Dora," Diego said, thinking that maybe this was his cousin's idea of an elaborate prank, maybe some way of getting back at him for the whole dance thing.

"What?" Sammy said. "We're not on a plane; we can't . . . Oh, we're on a plane. We've left the country without ID! We need to alert the US Consulate!"

While Sammy ranted, Randy tapped the screen on his smartphone. "I don't have any signal," he said, panic in his voice. "No, no, no, no! This can't be happening!"

"That's your worry right now?" Diego said, pointing at Randy's phone.

"I can't handle this much reality!" Randy replied.

Diego got up and looked out a hole to see for himself. "What airport is this?" he wondered.

"All I see is jungle. Why are we in the jungle?" Sammy asked, knowing only that of all the places that she would want to be right now, the jungle was most certainly not one of them.

"Dora?" Diego asked. "What happened?"

Dora knew they had come for her. They needed her parents to find Parapata. She turned to face her cousin and spoke in Spanish. *"Vinieron por mi. ¡Están tras mis padres! ¡Después de Parapata!"*

"Parapata?!" Diego said in disbelief. He thought Dora was joking. *"¿En serio?"*

"¡Son cazadores de tesoros!" Sammy said, joining the conversation.

Randy wanted to smack himself in the head. "Why did I take Mandarin? What are you guys saying?!"

"They are treasure hunters. Mercenaries! After a legendary Inca lost city!" Diego exclaimed, this time in English.

Sammy suddenly leaned in toward Dora and Diego and, in the most pleasant, reasonable voice you could imagine, said, "I'm sorry . . . What did you say?"

Before anyone could answer, the crate was thrown about as it was being loaded onto the back of the flatbed truck. Everyone inside fell back to the floor.

"We've got to get out of here!" Diego said, which seemed like a pretty good idea to everyone.

Dora immediately went through her backpack, which of course she'd brought with her to the museum and into the crate because, hello, she's Dora, and she doesn't go ANY-WHERE without her backpack. A second later, she produced a military-grade Swiss Army knife.

"Dora brought a knife on the field trip, everybody," Sammy observed wryly.

Without taking the bait, Dora used the knife blade to pry the lid of the crate just enough so she could poke her head out. "We're on a flatbed truck," she said. "I see three mercenaries. Armed. Wait, there's a fourth!"

Dora's eyes were wild as she ducked her head back into the box. "He saw me! He's coming for us!"

Randy closed his eyes. "I'm not here," he said. "I'm not here. I'm an avatar. I'm an avatar."

Before he could say another word, the lid to the crate cracked open a little more, courtesy of a crowbar. A man looked inside the crate, staring right at Dora. He was kind of bookish, a little nerdy, maybe, and older, like maybe around the same age as Dora's dad.

The man took another look at Dora and said, "I didn't believe it! Dora! It *is* you! How did you get here?!"

"Who are you?" Dora asked in amazement.

"I'm a friend of your parents'!" he said, excited. "I'm rescuing you, Dora! Come with me if you want to l—"

Suddenly, the truck lurched forward, and before the man could say anything else, he was thrown backward.

"Where did he go?" Sammy asked.

"Did he die?" Randy wondered.

Then the man reappeared, and other than his hair looking all messed up, he seemed all right. "I'm okay! I need your help. But we have to run," the man said. "Now!"

❄ ❄ ❄

"Uh, boss?" said the woman security guard.

From the truck cabin, she checked her rearview mirror and saw them: a man, with four kids, running across the tarmac behind them. The delivery guy looked behind them as well and saw the five people sprinting toward a rickety-looking airplane hangar.

"How many did we kidnap?" asked the male security guard.

"Get them!" said the delivery guy.

Immediately, the mercenaries set off in pursuit. And the delivery guy whistled. But he wasn't whistling to another mercenary. He was whistling to, of all things . . .

. . . a fox. An actual, honest-to-goodness fox, wearing a mask.

"Whatever happens," the delivery guy said to the fox, "get that map!"

The fox seemed to understand this, and bounded from the truck, racing off after Dora and her companions.

✽ ✽ ✽

"What is happening?" Sammy said frantically. "My parents did not sign a permission slip for the jungle! Why are we here? Why? Why?"

Inside the hangar, Dora ran past some old airplanes, the kind that had engines with propellers, not the more modern jets. "How do we get out of here?" she said, looking at the weird, bookish man who had come to their rescue.

"I don't know!" he said. "Getting you out of the box was as far as my plan went!"

"What kind of rescue is this?" Diego asked, which seemed like a fair question to the other three kids.

The man looked annoyed. "It's the only one you've got!" he replied.

Suddenly, Dora threw open the hangar door. And as she did so, a sleek, fast-moving shape tore inside.

It was the fox!

And it completely freaked out the nice guy who had tried to rescue Dora and her friends.

The fox grabbed at Dora's backpack, pulling it away from her. Executing a backflip, the fox landed on the roof of a prop plane and started to rifle through the backpack.

Until it found the map.

"That fox swiped my map!" Dora shouted. "We have to stop him!"

Everyone just looked at her like she had five heads.

"What part of 'That fox swiped my map' don't you understand?" she thundered. "Help me!"

Before anyone could do anything, the fox had snatched the map between its teeth and sprinted along the wings of the prop plane upon which it had landed. Then it leaped from one plane to another, racing along its wings, then leaping to another, and so on.

Dora was off like a leopard.

"Where is she going?!" shouted the nice man with approximately 10 percent of a rescue plan.

"Dora!" Diego shouted.

But it was too late. Dora was right there behind the fox, leaping from plane to plane. "No swiping, you . . . you . . . swiper!" Dora screamed.

Then the fox hopped onto the engine mount of an old airplane, which in turn caused the propeller to spin around. Dora would certainly have run right into it, if she hadn't slid right under it in the nick of time.

"Holy crap!" Randy said, stunned. "She's amazing!"

"We have to do something!" Diego said. Turning around, Diego saw that Mr. 10 Percent of a Rescue Plan was running away in the opposite direction from the action. Not fast by Diego's standards, but probably pretty fast by that guy's.

"No, no, no, no, no, no, no," the man said, his voice growing fainter as he ran away.

"Well, that's not very brave," Sammy observed.

Meanwhile, something interesting had occurred in the battle of wills between Dora and the fox. The propeller

had kept on spinning, and the fox was now stuck on it. He couldn't go anywhere. Dora just stared at him.

"Stop, you swiper!" Dora said again. Then she stopped the propeller from spinning, which caused the fox to fly right off over her shoulder. "Oh, shoot! Swiper, no swiping!"

Racing after the fox, who still had the map clutched in his teeth, Dora rounded a corner, only to slam right into the three mercenaries! They came right for Dora as she stood her ground.

"Dora! No!" Diego cried out.

"I need my map!" Dora protested. "It's my friend!"

That was a weird thing to say, wasn't it? But trust us, there's weirder stuff to come.

Dora turned around and saw Diego holding open a side door. "Come on! Now!" he shouted. This might be Dora's only chance to escape, even if it was without the map.

❋ ❋ ❋

Outside the hangar, Dora found herself running right alongside Diego, Sammy, and Randy.

"Now what do we do?" Sammy asked.

"Where did our rescuer go?" Dora wondered.

"He ran away," Randy replied.

"Yup," Diego added. "Totally ditched us."

Dora's heart sank for just a moment, until she heard the sound of a vehicle pulling up behind them. Looking around, she saw a beat-up old Land Rover, and in the driver's seat, Mr. 10 Percent of a Rescue Plan.

"Get in!" he ordered, just as the hangar door burst open.

"Don't let them escape!" screamed the delivery guy.

Dora didn't need an antelope, which is a very heavy animal, to fall on her. She got right on the Land Rover, along with the other kids. Soon as they did, their rescuer put the pedal to the metal, and they took off in a cloud of dust, leaving some very unhappy, empty-handed mercenaries behind.

CHAPTER 9

A FEW MINUTES LATER, the Land Rover was putting more and more distance between Dora and her friends, and the mercenaries. That was the good news. The bad news was, the mercenaries—specifically that swiping fox—had Dora's map.

"Hold on!" cried Mr. 10 Percent of a Rescue Plan, who, in all fairness, should probably be called Mr. 50 Percent of a Rescue Plan now, maybe more, on account of the Land Rover escape. He was taking them through jungle foliage and onto what you might barely describe as a dirt "road."

"Are they following?" he asked, "they" meaning the mercenaries.

Dora looked behind her. She didn't see anything. But then she heard a low rumble. Everyone in the Land Rover ducked. On another road, Dora heard the sound of the flatbed truck, the one that the mercenaries were going to use to transport Dora and her friends who knows where.

"Not anymore," Diego said, and everyone heaved a sigh of relief that the mercenaries had missed them.

For now.

"Are you kids okay?" Mr. 50 Percent of a Rescue Plan asked.

Right on cue, Randy leaned over the side of the vehicle and threw up. "Not really," he said.

"'Not really?'" Sammy said. "Understatement of the

century! I was just kidnapped! And chased by bad guys! And a fox. With a mask. Everyone saw that, right? Like, why does that fox need to remain anonymous? Who's going to recognize one specific fox?"

It was a good question.

Another good question was about to come, and Dora had it. "How do you know my name?" she asked Mr. 50 Percent of a Rescue Plan.

"You were an infant the last time I saw you," he said. "My name is Alejandro Gutierrez. I'm a professor of ancient languages at San Marcos University in Lima. I work with your parents. I fear they're in trouble."

"I know!" Dora said. "Those guys on the plane are after my parents!"

Alejandro (who we're glad not to refer to as "Mr. 50 Percent of a Rescue Plan" anymore) nodded. "Your parents and I were in constant contact during their time here. Then, two weeks ago, your parents' calls stopped. Since then, *silencio*."

Sammy looked right at Randy and said, "That means 'silence.'"

"Yeah, I got that one," Randy replied, still feeling queasy.

"They haven't answered any of my sat phone calls for weeks, either!" Dora said, comparing notes with Alejandro.

"In their last message, they said they'd hit a dead end in their search for Parapata," Alejandro continued. "A puzzle they couldn't solve. A riddle. A mystery. An enigma. A quandary—"

"Okay, we get it!" Sammy interjected, stopping Alejandro

from going through the complete list of synonyms for "puzzle." "They got a thing they couldn't do!"

Alejandro seemed grateful. "That's what I meant. Exactly!" Then he pulled something out from the Land Rover and showed it to Dora. "Your father sent me this just the week before, in case I could help."

"Papi's journal . . ." Dora said softly.

"So I came here to make sure they were okay. Tracked them this far. I've been staking it out, hoping for a sign from them, and then . . . I saw you poke your head out of that crate, and I said to myself, 'Dora! Dora the . . . kidnapped teenager! It cannot be!'" Alejandro said quickly, barely taking a breath as he spoke.

Dora decided that she didn't like "Dora the kidnapped teenager" so much. It didn't have the same ring as "Dora the explorer," which almost rhymed.

"But how did you recognize me?" Dora asked.

Alejandro didn't know what else to say. "Well, you look sort of exactly the same," he said. "But I'm afraid I have no idea where to find your parents."

"And that fox, um, Swiper . . . took your map," Diego said.

That particular fact didn't seem to be bothering Dora. "Don't worry about that," she said. "I can track my parents in the jungle. They'll have left markings and footprints! And we have Papi's journal!"

The missing map still bothered Alejandro, though. "But those mercenaries will have a head start with the stolen map," he argued.

"Then we better hurry," Dora suggested. "Let's go!"

Sammy raised her hands. "Hold up!" she said. "Or we could call the local police and have them come rescue us with, like, a SWAT team!"

Randy nodded. "That sounds like another solid option," he said.

This clearly didn't sound like a "solid option" to Alejandro. "'Hello? Nine-one-one? Can you please come and get us? We're at the corner of Rain and Forest.' Do you see any local police?" he asked. "Do you see any *locals*? There is nothing here. There is only . . . jungle."

Sammy didn't appreciate being mocked. But even more than that, she didn't appreciate the situation in which she found herself. "I get it!" she said tersely. "I just want to go home!"

"The fastest way home is for us to find my parents," Dora said. "They'll know what to do. The jungle is where I am from. I've got this. Trust me."

"Trust you?" Sammy said, balking. "I trusted you to find a clue on a scavenger hunt, and I ended up kidnapped and in a jungle on the other side of the world! I was worried you were going to be a threat. But you're actually the dumbest person I've ever met!"

Now it was Randy's turn to freak out a little. "We're gonna die out here!" he said, wigging. "Look around you! This is the kind of place where people die!"

They might have been freaking, but none of it fazed Dora. "I mean, in a way, every place is the kind of place where people die," she said, trying to find the bright side.

Except, you know, there was no bright side.

"Okay, well, that's a bummer notion," Sammy said.

"Finding Dora's parents is our best chance of getting home," Alejandro said, agreeing with Dora. "The only other way out is a five-hundred-mile walk through deep, virgin jungle with killer bugs, snakes, and piranha."

In unison, Sammy, Randy, and Diego looked into the jungle.

"My aunt and uncle will know what to do," Diego said, suddenly backing his cousin. "I'm mad at Dora, too. But she is my cousin. I can't let her go off by herself with this strange and anxious man we just met."

"Thank you, Diego," Alejandro said, maybe not realizing exactly the noncompliment he had just been paid. "Now let's go find Dora's parents!"

He threw the car into gear, and they took off once more into the jungle.

CHAPTER 10

THE LAND ROVER WAS making
pretty good time through the jungle, all things
considered. "All things considered" being the world's worst,
most pothole-ridden dirt road, some very bitey mosquitos,
and heat so extreme that it made hot seem cold.

That last one makes sense if you think about it. Sort of.

Anyway.

A couple of hours had past as the crew ventured down the
dirt road, when Dora suddenly shouted out. "Look!" she said,
motioning toward some bushes up ahead. "In there! That's
their car!"

The Land Rover pulled up alongside the bushes. Hidden
inside was a beat-up old Jeep. Alejandro threw the Land
Rover into park, and he and Dora hopped out to investigate.

"We should search their car and see if they left any clues,"
he said.

Dora looked around, and almost immediately saw the
familiar red *O* painted on a tree in berry juice. The little
glimmer of hope she had been holding inside started to grow.
"Here! This is it!" she said. "Our family symbol. In case of
emergency, we leave it. Like a trail of bread crumbs. They
started hiking here . . ."

Sammy hopped from the Land Rover and walked over to

Dora. "Are we there? Where are your parents? I don't see your parents," she said impatiently.

"We can't go any farther by car," Dora said, which was not news that anyone wanted to hear. "The jungle gets too dense."

"So how do we . . ." Diego started.

"We must enter the jungle on foot," Alejandro said, picking up from Dora. "Luckily, I prepared for this possibility."

Alejandro then showed everyone his "preparation" when he opened the hatch on the back of the Land Rover, revealing an abundance—an overabundance, actually—of supplies. The only thing that was immediately recognizable as remotely helpful was a huge quantity of instant oatmeal. The other stuff, like ski masks and DVD box sets of popular movies? That was less obviously helpful.

Before anyone could say anything, Alejandro said, "I may have gone a little overboard on supplies. Costco just has everything!"

The kids looked through the mountain of stuff and succeeded in finding some useful supplies, like food, and shoved it all into backpacks.

While they did that, Dora got busy gathering some branches. "We need to cover our tracks," she said, and proceeded to cover the Land Rover and her parents' Jeep with the branches.

Then Diego, Randy, Sammy, and Alejandro approached the path they would be taking into the dense jungle. It was, in a word, scary.

"This is a legit nightmare," Sammy said, and she wasn't wrong.

Then Randy went to pat his pocket and immediately realized something was missing. "Wait!" he cried. "I can't find my phone. I lost my phone! We have to go back. We can split into two search parties. My phone is somewhere between here and the airport. Guys?"

Everyone looked at Randy.

Then everyone ignored Randy.

"There's no time to waste," Alejandro said. "I'm not going first, though. You go first, Dora, it feels right. *Tengo miedo.*"

Dora summoned her courage and prepared to take a step forward. Then she turned back. "You all have nothing to worry about," she said to the group. "The jungle is perfectly safe. Just don't touch anything. Or breathe too deeply."

Randy felt queasy again.

✽ ✽ ✽

About the only predictable thing you can say about the jungle is that it's unpredictable. Dora knew that, but her friends were just learning that hard fact when the downpour started.

As if making their way through dense, unforgiving jungle wasn't enough, now they had to contend with hard, driving rain. It wasn't something that Diego, Sammy, Randy, or even Alejandro remotely enjoyed.

But Dora? The rain didn't seem to bother her in the slightest. In fact, she was singing.

"We're on our way!
On a jungle adventure
Now we gotta gotta
Save my parents!
So we're walking walking
In the rain!"

Alejandro had no idea what to make of it. He turned to Diego and asked, "Is this normal behavior for her?"

Diego rolled his eyes. "I forgot it could be so hot and so wet," he said, ignoring the question, preferring to focus on how uncomfortable the jungle was.

That was Randy's cue to chime in with the complaining. "It's like the air is sweating and that sweat is sweating, and—"

"We get it, Randy," Sammy said, cutting him off.

Trying to change the subject, Alejandro said, "Does anyone need a bathroom break? That's a thing adults ask kids, right?"

This seemed entirely reasonable, and so the kids went off into the jungle to go to the bathroom (which is a weird thing to say, considering there was no actual bathroom there, but you get our point). Everyone went, except for Sammy.

"You need to go?" Dora asked her on the sly.

"No, thanks," Sammy replied, clearly not wanting to talk about it. "I'm good. I'm good."

Dora shrugged, and the group pressed on through the deep jungle.

CHAPTER 11

ANOTHER COUPLE OF HOURS

passed, and it was starting to get dark. The
group had been listening to animal sounds, insect noises,
and the rustling wind all afternoon. But as darkness
descended, everything started to take on an even more ominous tone.

You know what didn't help that feeling? It might have
been the bundles of sticks they found hanging from the trees
as they kept on walking. Or the fact that mixed in with the
sticks were animal bones.

And then there was the Inca sun symbol that was on each
of these bundles.

They made everyone nervous.

They made Sammy especially nervous. "Okay, what are
these?" she asked.

Dora said, "Nothing," just playing it off.

"Warning signs," Alejandro said, assuring Sammy that
they were, in fact, something. "Totems."

It all felt very creepy, and the group tried to go forward
and remain as quiet as possible while doing so. There was the
inescapable feeling that they were being watched, and not by
the mercenaries, but by someone, or something, else.

"Wait, what?" Randy said, just picking up on Alejandro's
words. "Like 'Don't trespass'?"

"More like 'Stop now or you'll be cursed forever,'" he answered.

Something in the bushes moved, and Sammy jumped.

"Seriously?" she said, angry. "Cursed? Cursed? By whom?"

Alejandro wasn't sure if he should say anything. "Legend tells of a deadly ancient militia dedicated to protecting Parapata from outside eyes," he said.

Randy was riveted. "Legend like a unicorn, or legend like Zelda?"

Alejandro was confused. "Those are both legends. Wait, do you think one of those is real?" he asked Randy.

Embarrassed, Randy shrugged, pulled down his hoodie, and tried to turn invisible.

"No one has seen Los Guardianes Perdidos, the Lost Guardians, for centuries," Alejandro said, giving a name to the unseen forces that could possibly be tracking their every move.

Just then, Dora said something in a language that no one in the group understood.

"What was that?" Diego asked his cousin.

"Quechua," Alejandro said, making it one person who understood. "Ancient Inca. Impressive."

"What does it mean?" Sammy asked.

"'All those that seek Parapata shall surely perish,'" Alejandro said. The group fell quiet.

"Okay," Randy spoke up. "I think I'm ready for my parents to come get me now."

"What exactly is this Parapata?" Sammy asked, really curious now.

"Is it like a chupacabra or something?" Randy said, his voice tinged with fear.

"Parapata is a legendary Inca city, lost long ago," Dora said, trying to allay Randy's fears.

Suddenly, Diego remembered something from the times he'd spent with Dora and her family when they were much younger. "'The City of Gold,'" Diego said.

"Gold?" Randy asked.

"Like half the gold," Alejandro clarified.

"Half of what?" Randy said.

"Spanish legends tell us that over half the world's supply of gold lies in Parapata. Enough gold to forge a statue larger than the Statue of Liberty," Alejandro said.

That got everyone's attention. There was a collective "Whoa."

"Exactly," Alejandro finished.

"So think of the warnings as a good thing!" Dora said. "It means we're on the right track!"

This made exactly no one feel better, and only served to annoy the other kids.

Alejandro picked up on this and did his best to make them feel better. "You have nothing to worry about," he said, trying to sound reassuring. "At all. I promise. There is no need to overreact."

Which was a great speech, but probably not the best moment for him to step through a giant spiderweb.

"Ahhhhhhh!" Alejandro hollered. "Get it off me!"

He ran back and forth, grabbing at the sticky mass, trying

to get the web off of him. He kept running around, until finally, he smacked right into a low-lying tree branch.

"And that," he said, dusting himself off, "is an example of the dangers of overreacting."

✿ ✿ ✿

The group forged ahead, and was making real progress in their journey, despite the dark and foreboding jungle that engulfed them. Just when it seemed as if the foliage might swallow them whole, they came to a clearing. The sky was at last visible, no longer covered by the canopy of trees. But as dark as the night sky was, the jungle seemed even darker.

"We should camp here for the night, continue in the morning," Dora said. She had spent enough years living in the jungle to know when it was best to quit for the day and get some rest.

"Perhaps we should push on," Alejandro countered. "Your parents might not be too far ahead."

Diego jumped in. "You never explore the jungle at night. Even I remember that."

Dora looked at her cousin, and a faint smile crossed her face.

"Ah!" cried Randy, and everyone jumped. "I felt my phone ring. Anyone else having ghost phone?" he said, referring to that weird, phantom feeling people sometimes get in their leg that the phone in their pocket is vibrating, even though there's no phone there. "What I'd give to just sit down and stare at my phone for like four solid hours."

Alejandro sighed. It didn't look like they would be moving on. So he rummaged through the supplies. "Well, I only have

three hammocks," he said. "You kids can pair up."

Before anyone could speak, Sammy said, "I'm sleeping solo." That came out as a statement of immovable fact.

"Diego, you can bunk with me," Dora said. "It'll be like old times."

That left Randy and Alejandro to share a hammock, which clearly didn't thrill Alejandro. But, hey, beggars couldn't be choosers.

❋ ❋ ❋

No one was tired yet, despite the thoroughly exhausting day everyone had endured. So they made a small campfire and huddled around it, eating some of the ninety-five gajillion PowerBars that Alejandro had brought with him. They sat quietly and watched as Randy moved his thumbs in the air strangely, as if he were texting or playing a game on a nonexistent phone.

"I don't like it out here," Randy said, breaking the silence. "It's too quiet. But it's also not quiet enough. It's like, I also hate the insect and the animal noises, and also it's way too dark. And I hate how fresh the air smells. And how everything is wet . . ."

There was a collective feeling that Randy might go on like this all night. Dora patted him on the shoulder and then did something unexpected. She pulled out a smooth, slim, shiny rock, and placed it into Randy's "texting" hands.

"It's a river rock," Dora said. "I found it earlier and thought it might help."

"This is very embarrassing for your generation," said Alejandro.

Randy said nothing and just stared at the rock in his hands.

"You have to use your imagination!" Dora chided.

Randy took it in and, a few seconds later, started to work his thumbs up and down the rock, just as if it were a real phone. "You know," he started to say, "I know it's stupid, but this actually does make me feel better. Thanks, Dora."

With that, Alejandro turned to face Dora. "I hate to say it, but it's probably good you're here, Dora," he admitted. "I am almost assuredly not the right man for this mission."

"Person," Sammy corrected. "You're not the right *person* for the mission."

"But you are here, Alejandro," Dora said, sounding hopeful. "That means something. Plus, we each care about Parapata. And my parents. How long have you worked with them?"

"Years now," Alejandro said, shifting in his seat. "Mostly in a research capacity. I used to be great in the jungle, but then I left, and now I seem to have lost that part of me."

Dora looked at Alejandro, and her face was full of concern.

"Still," he continued, "I have to say, it seems as though you've trained your whole life for this mission, Dora. I'm surprised your parents didn't take you along with them."

Staring into the fire, Dora said nothing at first. "Me, too," Dora said. "I guess it was just . . ."

Her voice trailed off, and before she could complete her

thought, Sammy let out a gasp. She was staring right at Alejandro, and soon, everyone was staring at him.

Well, not at *him*, exactly. More like staring at the enormous stick bug that was climbing up Alejandro's arm and onto his neck.

"There's a giant insect on me, isn't there?" he asked.

Everyone nodded.

Alejandro started to breathe faster and faster. "Can someone please remove it before I pass out?" he begged.

As everyone stared, Dora calmly reached out and picked up the stick bug. "There you go, little friend, on your way!" she said cheerfully. *"Vamonos!"*

"Okay, this day is over," Alejandro said, and then he really did pass out.

❋ ❋ ❋

With Alejandro asleep, everyone else decided it was time to turn in as well. Randy joined Alejandro in the hammock, and Sammy took her own. That left Diego and Dora, who struggled to get comfortable and get at least a couple of hours' sleep before they had to be off on their trek once more.

"We used to share hammocks all the time," Dora said softly. "Remember?"

"I don't know," Diego said, a little grumpy. "I guess."

"We would stare up at the stars and try to identify constellations," Dora continued.

"I don't know," Diego repeated. "I guess."

"And you would always say that that constellation looked just like the two of us," Dora said, pointing up at the sky.

Strangely enough, the constellation kinda sorta did look like Diego and Dora, if you connected the stars in a certain way.

"I don't know," Diego said once more. "I guess."

Despite Diego's indifference, Dora went on. "And we would just lie there and talk and talk until one of us fell asleep, usually you."

"I don't know. I guess."

"Except for that one time a boa grabbed you like this!" And with that, Dora brought her arm around Diego and grabbed his leg hard.

Diego screamed. "Ahhhh! Boa!" He started to flip around in the hammock, trying to escape the clutches of the deadly, thoroughly nonexistent "boa." Then Dora expertly flipped the hammock over, causing Diego to fall right out and onto the ground below.

"You did that on purpose!" he accused.

"I don't know," Dora said, imitating her cousin. "I guess . . ."

Diego gazed into Dora's eyes, angry. But he couldn't keep being angry, not at her. So he started to laugh.

So did Dora.

"You got me, *prima*," Diego said. Dora offered her hand to him, pulling Diego back up.

CHAPTER 12

AFTER THE GROUP HAD what approached a decent night's sleep, they gathered their gear and set off on their jungle trek once more. Dora noticed immediately that Sammy seemed to be walking a little funny, and sidled up next to her.

"You okay?" Dora asked.

"Fine, totally fine," Sammy said, in a way that said, she wasn't fine, but don't ask. "Just keep on hacking away the jungle brush."

That's what the group had been doing all morning long, it seemed. Hacking away at the lush jungle growth, trying to follow the path of Dora's parents. Randy, still basking in the glow of his new rock phone, was busy hacking away with everyone else.

"Um, I found one of those red loops!" he shouted.

Dora raced over and took a look. Randy had revealed a tree behind some brush, and sure enough, there was the familiar red *O* drawn in red berry juice.

"My parents' symbol," she said.

"We must be getting close," Alejandro offered.

Sammy looked like she was about to fall down on her knees and kiss the ground. "Oh, thank you, thank you, thank you!" she exclaimed.

Dora seized the initiative and barreled headlong through the jungle.

✽ ✽ ✽

When they emerged from the brush, Dora was greeted by a sight that was at once welcome and unwelcome.

"This is my parents' camp," she said. "Or was. This is their stuff . . ."

Sure enough, all evidence suggested that the place was once a campsite. But it was now in total disarray, as if someone had been there and searched it thoroughly, leaving no sleeping bag or backpack unturned. Dora noticed that throughout the campsite, there were heavy footprints, made by what looked like combat boots.

"What kind of animal did this?" Randy asked.

"These are Australian Army standard-issue Redback Terra prints," Dora answered.

"Redback Terra prints," Alejandro echoed.

"Size forty-five," Dora added.

"Size forty-five," Alejandro parroted.

"Popular with mercenaries."

"Popular with mercenaries. Good job, us! We did it!" Alejandro said.

Diego took a moment to examine the ground around him. He noticed some small marks that resembled tiny little footprints.

"And these," Diego said slowly, "are fox tracks. Wait, how do I know that?"

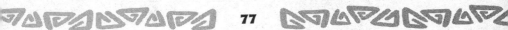

Dora smiled at her cousin. "Because you are an expert on all types of animals!" she reminded him.

"I still think you're confusing me with someone else," Diego replied, even though a part of him was starting to believe what Dora said was true.

"This looks really bad for your parents," Randy said, clearly worried. "I mean, I can't imagine anyone survived this; just look . . ."

At that moment, Randy looked up, and noticed that everyone was staring right at him. Each face had the same look, which seemed to say, *YOU NEED TO STOP TALKING RIGHT NOW.*

"I'm sure they're okay, Dora," Diego said, trying to reassure his cousin.

"Yeah," Sammy said, then glared at Randy. "He's still getting used to talking to people in real life."

Randy nodded in agreement. Dora looked around the campsite a little while longer, then said, "My parents are okay. There are two sets of footprints. They were gone before the mercenaries arrived, but they left in a hurry."

Alejandro leaned down next to Dora and looked at the tracks she had mentioned. "But this means the mercenaries are ahead of us," he said, a grave tone in his voice. "We'll have to quicken our pace."

They were just about ready to set off on the trail of Dora's parents when there came a rustling sound. Immediately, down to the person, they froze in their tracks.

"Or they're still here," Diego said in a hushed voice.

78

"Someone is watching," Sammy whispered. "I can feel it!"

"Where's my stone phone?" Randy said. "My iStone?"

He reached into his pocket, fumbled around, and found the stone. Randy grasped it tight in his hand, and found that it gave him some comfort. Then he joined the other four as they formed a tight circle, standing back-to-back. This way, they could see anything coming from any direction.

There came another rustle of leaves.

"Kill it!" Alejandro shouted, without even seeing what it was. "Kill it quickly!"

And then something leaped right at them!

"Boots!" Dora exclaimed as she hugged the monkey tight to her chest. "Oh, Boots, I'm so happy to see you!"

You could practically hear everyone in the group sigh, glad that it wasn't a trained mercenary or a jungle cat ready to rip out their throats.

"She knows the monkey," Sammy said. "Of course she knows the monkey."

"Boots! I haven't seen you in . . ." Diego said, unable to contain his childlike excitement. His voice trailed off, as he suddenly remembered he wanted to play it cool. "I mean, sup, monkey."

Boots didn't seem to appreciate Diego's last comment, and shot him a disapproving look.

"Have you seen Mami and Papi?" Dora asked Boots.

"Why is she asking the monkey?" Alejandro wondered aloud.

No one answered, except Boots, who chattered away at

Dora. It was all noise to everyone else, but to Dora, it was the exact opposite. "Oh, thank goodness. He saw them!" Dora said, then she turned to face the group. "This is Boots. Boots, these are my friends. They're here to help me."

Sammy immediately corrected Dora. "No, we're here to get saved. And FYI, we are *not* friends."

Before Sammy could say another word, Boots jumped right onto her shoulder.

"Okay, there's a monkey on me," she said, unnerved.

Then Boots started to pick through Sammy's hair with his fingers.

"What's he doing?" Sammy said, jumpy.

"He's grooming you," Dora said proudly. "It's a sign of love and respect. And also hunger."

Boots continued to pick through Sammy's hair, looking for bugs to eat. He found something that looked surprisingly yummy and popped it in his mouth. Then he started to gag. Sammy reached her hands up to her hair.

"Where's my hair clip?" she asked.

"I'm afraid he has eaten it," Dora said. "But do not worry. I shall make sure to dig it out of his scat later."

And on that particularly gross note, Boots jumped off of Sammy and back to Dora. Then he motioned with his arms toward a nearby tree.

"What's that, Boots?" Dora asked her friend. She followed him over to the tree and saw another familiar red *O* written in berry juice. But this one wasn't as nice and neat as the

others Dora had seen. This one looked like it had been made in a hurry.

"They did this quickly," Dora said, urgency in her voice. "See how they rushed it? Still . . . I can track my parents better than those mercenaries. We just have to get to them first!"

"And we will, Dora," Alejandro said. "I have complete confidence in you."

Dora smiled up at Alejandro. It was exactly what she needed to hear at that moment. Summoning her considerable courage, she led the group back into the jungle.

❊ ❊ ❊

"May we stop for a moment?" Sammy called out. "I need to do a thing."

They had been on the jungle path for at least an hour, still following the trail left by Dora's parents. The group had been moving at a rapid pace, trying to beat the mercenaries. They were due for a quick two-minute break.

"What?" Randy said, noticing that Sammy had just stopped in her tracks.

"Just a thing," Sammy said.

"What is the thing?" Diego asked.

"I know what this is," Dora said, because of course she did. "You have to poo."

Sammy looked livid. "No. That isn't it," she insisted.

Dora and Sammy locked eyes.

A second passed, then another.

"Of course I have to poo!" Sammy blurted. "I haven't

pooed in forty-eight hours! I'm sweating, and every step is agony!" Then she turned to Diego and Randy. "Don't look at me! Cover your ears!"

Diego grimaced. "You should have said 'cover your ears' before you said 'poo' like a hundred times."

"No need to be afraid," Dora said, wanting to comfort Sammy. "I have an idea! Let's turn this into a song!"

This sounded like a terrible idea to Sammy, but she was in no position to argue. Dora grabbed her hand and led her away from the group. Boots hopped onto Dora's shoulder to keep tabs on his friend.

Once they were far enough away, Dora started to sing:

> "It's time to dig the poo hole!
>> Dig!
>>> Dig!
>>>> Dig!"

Then Dora pulled something from her backpack and, with a few flips and snaps, assembled a small shovel.

"Seriously?" Sammy said. "You had that in your backpack, too?"

"Poo shovel," Dora explained. Then she started to dig a hole in the ground, doing what appeared to be a little dance as she went around. Boots followed her, mimicking the dance.

> "Dig the poo hole!
>> Dig!
>>> Dig!
>>>> Dig!

Just grab a shovel!
It's a piece of cake!
Make sure the hole is deep!
And there isn't a snake!

Yeah!"

A moment later, Dora was finished, and Sammy looked at the ground in horror.

"I believe in you, Sammy," Dora said. "I believe you can do this. Also, medically, you *have* to do this."

Then Dora and Boots left Sammy, and that's about all we're going to say about that.

❋ ❋ ❋

"She's good," Dora said, gesturing toward the area where she had left Sammy. "There's nothing to be afraid of—"

As she spoke, an arrow soared right past her head, lodging itself with a loud **THUNK** into a tree trunk right next to Alejandro. He stared at the arrow, his eyes opening wider and wider.

"Not good," Alejandro said. "Not good at all."

Then a volley of arrows flew at them from all different directions.

"Go! Go! Go!" Dora shouted, motioning for everyone to move.

"Real arrows flying at us! Real arrows flying at us!" Randy screamed.

"Run!" Dora ordered.

And run they did, shuttling into the jungle, racing through

the thick brush, pushing branches aside with their arms, doing everything they could to get away from the arrows.

❋ ❋ ❋

Sammy was just finishing up when suddenly Diego, Dora, Alejandro, and Randy burst through the brush, running at full tilt.

"What is happening?!" she shouted as arrows whizzed right past her head. She sprinted off, following the others.

"It's the mercenaries!" Dora replied.

"Mercenaries don't use arrows!" Alejandro said. "They use bullets!"

"It's the curse!" Randy said with the certainty of a kid who uses a rock for a phone. "The curse is gonna perish us! We're gonna perish all over the place!"

Arrows continued to fly, just missing them, but getting closer with every shot.

THWACK!

THUNK!

THWACK!

"We're sitting ducks out here!" Sammy said. "We're too exposed!"

Looking up ahead, Diego saw something promising. "There!" he hollered. "Follow me!"

Diego made it to a huge, hollow, moss-covered tree that was lying on the ground. The group got Diego's idea immediately, and one by one, they crammed inside the tree trunk, taking cover from the arrows.

The tree trunk provided some shelter, but not much.

Whoever was hunting the group saw them crawl inside as arrows started to pierce the rotten wood.

THWACK!

THUNK!

As the arrows hit, they created little pinholes that allowed the jungle light to enter.

THUNK!

Another arrow hit, this time piercing Randy's backpack. It pinned him to the other side of the trunk.

"I'm hit!" Randy screamed, and turned to see some kind of red liquid dripping from his bag. "They got me! I'm bleeding out! I'm losing life force!"

"Oh no!" Alejandro said, panic in his voice. "I don't do well with blood!"

Alejandro looked like he was about to hurl. Then Diego ripped open Randy's backpack and pulled something out.

"It's a juice box," Diego said, showing it to Randy. "Just a juice box!"

"Oh, thank goodness," Alejandro said, relieved. "I was almost sick."

"I was almost dead!" Randy said.

THWACK!

THUNK!

THUNK!

More arrows pierced the trunk.

"I think we're safe for now," Alejandro said.

Which is something they weren't. As the arrows kept coming, one of them managed to catch a branch on the

top of the tree trunk. The branch moved with the arrow's momentum and started to tip the log over.

This wouldn't have been a problem, except for the fact that what no one realized was that the trunk was resting on top of a hill.

A very steep hill.

"Not safe! Not safe!" Alejandro screamed as the tree trunk started to roll down the hill with everyone inside!

CHAPTER 13

GOOD NEWS: AT LEAST the arrows weren't hitting the tree trunk anymore.

Bad news: Yeah, they were still rolling down a hill toward certain doom.

The trunk kept on rolling, bouncing along the knotted jungle floor, throwing everyone inside this way and that.

The trunk broke through some foliage before it finally crashed onto some rocks that stopped it entirely and came to rest on the bank of a river.

One by one, the group helped one another out from the trunk. They all looked dizzy, dinged up, and entirely the worse for wear. But they were alive.

"I can't say for sure, because I'm fairly confident I just sustained a brain injury," Alejandro mused, "but I do believe we may have just met Los Guardianes Perdidos. The Lost Guardians."

"I thought they were just a legend," Diego said.

"I guess they were a legend like Zelda, and after us," Randy said.

"Zelda's not re— Oh, forget it," Alejandro said, dropping it.

As Randy pulled the arrow from his juice box, Dora calmly walked over and examined it. She saw a sun symbol on the arrow.

"It's the same Inca sun symbol that was on those totems,"

Dora said, referring to the objects they had seen earlier in their jungle adventure.

Randy took the arrow back. "So, what, these are like legit arrows?" he asked. "Like, 'kill people' arrows?"

Alejandro took the arrow from Randy and examined it himself. He appeared a little confused but said, "The markings are . . . quite authentic."

Dora noticed that Sammy was now sitting on the log with her head down. Something wasn't right. She walked over to Sammy.

"Are you okay?" Dora asked.

Sammy looked up at Dora, her eyes full of rage. "Okay?" she said. "OKAY? No, I am not okay, okay? Randy almost got killed! I almost died in a log! A. LOG!"

Dora was starting to get the idea that Sammy was really not thrilled at the way things had been going.

"I want to go home!" Sammy continued. "I want to be staring at my phone in an ice-cold room drinking a frozen coffee beverage! I know that makes me sound real basic, but that's what I want! And, by the way, the poo song lied! It was totally dangerous! Arrows rained down on me! I hate it here!"

Then Sammy stood straight up from the log and started to stalk off. She stopped for a second, then said, "And I can't even storm off because the jungle will eat me!"

No one said a word for a moment.

And then . . .

"Maybe a song will help?" Dora said.

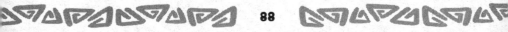 

"It's okay to freak out sometimes
It's fine to totally freak out . . ."

"NO! MORE! SONGS!" Sammy yelled.

"Finally, someone says what we're all thinking," Alejandro agreed.

Now it was Dora's turn to stalk off. But it wasn't so much stalking off as it was feeling guilty. Feeling guilty about everything that had happened.

Because she was sure it was all her fault.

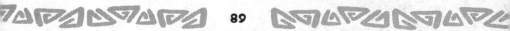

Dora was sitting on a log by herself, down by the riverbank. She didn't have much time to be alone, because Boots had followed her. He perched himself on her shoulder and did his best to console her.

Then she noticed someone else coming.

"Are you here to yell at me, too?" Dora asked.

Diego sat down beside her. "Nah," he said. "I'm just here to avoid getting yelled at by her, too." He gave his cousin a look that said, *What's up? You can talk to me.*

Dora took a deep breath. "It's scary to be responsible for other people," she said. "And to care about them. It's easier to be alone."

"She can be a real pain in the butt," Diego offered, "but she's not all bad, I guess."

And then Dora noticed it.

Diego smiled.

It was just a little smile, but still, it counted.

"Are you attracted to her?" Dora teased.

"Um, I definitely never said that," Diego protested.

"You know, a life-threatening situation often accelerates the mating process in many species," Dora continued.

"Okay, slow your roll," Diego said. "Also, please don't ever say 'mating' again."

He hopped up from the log and gestured over his shoulder. "Let's just get out of here. Are we even going the right way?"

Dora stood up and looked down at the ground, noticing something.

"What?" Dora asked. Dora knew immediately what she was looking at.

Diego knelt down beside her and as if reading her mind, he said the words out loud. "Fox tracks."

CHAPTER 14

IT WAS AN EASY matter for Dora
and Diego to follow the fox tracks. Dora had
spent her entire life preparing for just such a situation. And
for Diego, it was like the last ten years never happened, and
he was six years old again. All his knowledge and skills came
flooding back to him.

Peering through some foliage, Dora and Diego, with
Boots in tow, saw what looked like another campsite. But this
one didn't belong to Dora's parents.

This one belonged to the mercenaries.

And from the look of things, the mercenaries were getting
ready to head out.

As they listened, Dora and Diego overheard the mercenaries call each other by their names . . .

Viper (that was the security guard).

Christina X (that was the guard at the museum who
helped Dora).

Powell (the delivery guy).

"I scouted the area," Viper said. "There's a freshly cut path
to the north. Some ruins to the east."

Christina X chimed in, "Well, we know they came this
far." She nodded at a tree in the distance, marked with a red
O in berry juice.

Dora and Diego looked at each other and knew this meant trouble.

"This is the last marked coordinate on the map," Powell said. "You didn't find any more of their markings?"

Viper shrugged. "No. But there are some footprints on that path to the north. The rain could have washed the rest away. That's the path they took."

Powell gave a sharp nod. "Then we head north. We need to reach the Marquezes before those stupid kids warn them," he said.

Powell started down the path, with Viper and Christina X behind him.

"And if we don't?" Viper asked.

Christina X rolled her eyes. "Shut up, Viper," she said, sounding exasperated. "Boss'll take care of the kids if he has to."

"Hey, guys, what's going . . ."

Dora and Diego whipped their heads around, only to see an eager Alejandro right behind them, looking super clueless. They immediately gave him the biggest shushing of his life as Diego yanked him down to the ground and out of sight.

And then they sat super still, praying that no one had heard them.

"What was that?" Viper said.

Suddenly, Boots jumped out, grabbed a tree branch, and swung overhead, making an odd assortment of monkey noises. Then he stuck his tongue out at Powell before disappearing back into the jungle.

"You scared of monkeys now?" Powell taunted.

Meet
DORA

**Explorer. Adventurer.
Teenager.**

She's lived
her entire life in the
jungle, and she's become
an expert at discovering new
ways to uncover ancient
mysteries . . . and freak
out her parents.

"IF YOU JUST BELIEVE
IN YOURSELF, ANYTHING
IS POSSIBLE!"

With the help of her trusty map and backpack, Dora has no problem traversing through the thick jungles of South America.

Dora's mother and father are archaeologists. They've spent their entire careers searching for the lost city of Parapata. They worry about Dora when she goes on her adventures.

Dora's parents send her to the city to live with her cousin Diego. When Dora arrives at the airport, she is overwhelmed by the hustle and bustle of the city.

It's been ten years since Dora and Diego have seen each other. Dora is excited, but Diego tries his best to act cool.

"WE'RE GOING TO HAVE SO, SO MUCH FUN!"

It's Dora's first day at her new school. She meets a kid named Randy by the lockers. But Diego tries to tell Dora not to talk to Randy because he's a loser.

"DON'T LOOK AT ME LIKE I'M A JERK. I DON'T MAKE THE RULES HERE."

When Dora goes on a field trip to the museum, she gets paired up with Diego, Randy, and a girl named Sammy. Sammy is popular and an honor roll student.

Suddenly, Dora and her friends are kidnapped and taken back to the jungle by a group of mercenaries!

Dora and her friends are saved by Alejandro Gutierrez, a fellow explorer. Now they need to find Dora's parents. They stumble upon an abandoned opera house while on their journey.

Dora finds her parents! They've been looking for the lost city of Parapata. They are happy Dora is safe.

"DORA, YOU'RE OUR MOST IMPORTANT TREASURE. WE WOULD PROTECT YOU OVER ANYTHING."

The ancient ruins are one giant puzzle that leads to the lost city! Alejandro turns on Dora and her friends. He's used them this whole time to get into the city.

The golden monkey is the key to the puzzle. Alejandro makes a grave mistake and falls through a trap door. Dora knows the Incans treasured water above all else.

With the lost city safe from the mercenaries and her parents found, Dora and her friends head back to normal life. Only this time, Dora has three of the best friends any explorer could ask for.

"WE DID IT!"

"Monkeys can carry three times their body weight," Viper said defensively.

"So that's a yes?" Powell asked. "Viper is scared of monkeys?"

"It's just a fact," Viper said. "That's all it is."

Then Viper shrugged and followed Powell and Christina X away from their camp and onto a path that led into the jungle.

❋ ❋ ❋

As soon as the mercenaries were out of sight, Dora, Diego, and Alejandro were up and out from their hiding spot. They needed to meet back up with Randy and Sammy and keep on moving.

Walking along the path, Dora had her face buried in her father's journal.

"The mercenaries are ahead of us," Diego warned. "How are we supposed to get to your parents first now?"

Alejandro shook his head. "We can't. We'll just have to follow them from a safe distance," he said sadly.

But Dora wasn't having it. "No, we're not following them," she said stubbornly. "My parents didn't go that way."

Turning a page in the journal, Dora showed Diego and Alejandro a sketch of an old, ornate opera house located in the middle of the jungle.

"My father says the way to Parapata passes through an opera house," Dora said. "The mercenaries mentioned ruins to the east. The opera house was built hundreds of years ago by Europeans during the rubber boom. It would be nothing but ruins by now. I know my parents; that's the way they went."

There was no question about it, then.

They were off to find the opera house.

✿✿✿

"Doesn't look like any opera singers have been here in a while," Diego said.

The group was now standing in front of the old ruined opera house, which was exactly where Dora said it would be. It was crumbling, decrepit, covered in vines, and definitely creepy.

"The Europeans may have built it," Alejandro said, "but the jungle has taken it back."

Suddenly, someone started to sing, and guess what?

IT WASN'T DORA!

> **"The phaaaaaaaaantom of the opera is**
> **there, inside my mind!"**

It was Randy.

Singing showtunes.

In the middle of the jungle.

But he stopped singing abruptly, as he felt something weird beneath his feet.

"Why does the ground feel like chocolate pudding?" Sammy said, noticing the same thing.

Randy looked down and pulled his foot out of what looked like really thick mud. It made a loud noise that sounded like

SCHLORP

The noise made Randy laugh. So he did it again.

SCHLORP

"Ha! Excuse me! Check this out, guys!" Randy said, inviting everyone else to watch.

So he did the foot thing again and again. Finally, Diego decided to give it a shot.

SCHLORP

"Uh-oh," Diego said, laughing. "It must be catching! Pardon me!"

SCHLORP

Sammy and Dora joined in as well.

SCHLORP

"Must be something I ate, sorry!" Dora chuckled.

"Real mature, guys," Alejandro said. "Fart jokes? Really? We're stooping to fart jokes?"

Then Alejandro lifted his foot from the mud and made the biggest

SCHLORP

of them all.

"I deserve that." Alejandro laughed.

This went on for a while, until Randy noticed something a little odd about their situation.

"Anyone else notice the walls are getting higher?" Randy asked.

Everyone stopped laughing for a moment and looked around. More like they looked up. The walls weren't growing taller.

They were sinking.

"Quicksand!" Dora shouted.

CHAPTER 15

"YOU'VE GOT TO BE kidding me!" Alejandro yelled. "When is this day going to end?!"

"I can't move my legs!" Diego shouted.

"Quicksand really exists?" Randy asked. "I thought it was just a video game thing!"

Dora instantly assumed command of the situation. "Okay, rule number one of quicksand! Don't panic!" she ordered. "You'll only get sucked in farther!"

"She's right!" Sammy said. "Quicksand is just sand, clay, and water! And it's physically impossible to drown in it because it's twice as dense as your body! Eventually, you'll float!"

This was great news, except for the fact that everyone by now had sunken up to their waists in the sticky mess of mud.

"I'm definitely not floating," Alejandro said, panicking. "How do we get out of this stuff?!"

"Step one! Lie down on your back! You have to distribute your weight," Dora said.

Without a word, everyone immediately maneuvered so they were lying down on their backs.

"This feels super wrong," said Diego.

Dora ignored her cousin. "Now make little movements with your legs to make space for the water to get between the sand!" Dora said. "Once your legs are free, simply backstroke out of the quicksand."

"This is way too complicated," Alejandro said. "Just tell me how to get out of this!"

But Alejandro wasn't the only one having trouble. Sammy and Diego were also in a tough spot.

"This isn't working!" Sammy said.

"I'm losing feeling in my legs!" Diego added.

"Just do what I said and try to stay calm," Dora said. "We have to lower our heart rates. I know! We'll think of comforting things. I'll start."

"Okay, this is stupid now," Alejandro said.

"I'm going to think of my friends," Dora said. "Let's see, there's Boots. And Map. And there's Backpack."

She was quiet for a moment, and then said, "I guess the truth is . . . I don't really have any *human* friends right now. Or any real friends at all."

The quicksand pit fell silent again.

And then, one by one, each of the kids said, "Yeah, me neither."

Even Alejandro said, "Me neither."

"Well, this got depressing," Sammy said.

But in the time everyone was listening to Dora and getting depressed, Dora herself had managed to work her way to the edge of the quicksand pit. She slowly grabbed the edge and pulled herself out.

She was free!

"Look, it's working!" Randy cried out.

"That's because it's just as comforting to tell the truth!" Dora said. "It's cathartic! Someone else go, quick!"

Alejandro still wasn't convinced. "Oh, give me a break!" he complained. "We're going to die in here. What are you—"

"I've got one!" Randy interrupted. "When I was young, I used to pretend to drown at the public pool because the lifeguards would give me free juice boxes, but then they stopped giving me free juice boxes, 'cause they were scared I would really drown. Now I can hold my breath for seven minutes!"

And in the time it took him to tell that story, which probably seemed like seven minutes, Randy had made his way to the edge of the quicksand pit. With an assist from Dora, he was free now, too!

"Wow, we're really doing this, huh?" Diego said. "Fine! I found it really hard moving to the city when I was six! And I think I deny who I was then to make it easier for me now. I hate having to worry all the time about being cool. And I don't even like the people I try to impress! In fact, I kind of hate them!"

Diego had made it to safety, and now it was Sammy's turn.

"I know that everyone at school hates me," she said. "And that's fine. But what hurts is that no one even knows me. Nobody knows that my parents barely scrape by. That my clothes are all donations. That my family is drowning in debt. That's why I push myself. That's why I'm like this. Because it's all on me to make a better life for us."

Now Sammy was free as well, with Diego reaching out his hand to help. She was glad that he was there waiting for her.

"That got really real," she said to him.

The only one left now in the quicksand pit was Alejandro.

While the others had been telling their stories, and following Dora's rules, and escaping, Alejandro had just been wiggling and sinking. Now the only parts of him that were visible were his face and his chest.

"I'm not telling any stupid story, just pull me out of here!" Alejandro yelled. But he continued to panic, and so he sank even farther into the mud. Only his head poked out now.

But something behind him caught Dora's eye.

"Alejandro!" she called out to him. "You have to stop moving! Stay still!"

"What?" Alejandro asked. "What is it?"

Alejandro tried to turn his head, but was unable to due to the dense mud. But everyone else could see what Dora had noticed seconds before.

A scorpion.

"Why have you all gone quiet?" Alejandro asked. "What's behind me? It's bad, isn't it? If it wasn't bad, you would all be talking as much as you usually do!"

"Don't move a muscle!" Dora said, which was easy for Alejandro considering his current situation.

The scorpion scuttled along the mud, right in front of Alejandro.

"Ahhhhh!" he screamed. "I knew it! Go away! Shoo! Shoo!"

But the scorpion didn't shoo. Instead, it circled around Alejandro. Not knowing what else to do, Alejandro tried to blow it away.

Then a second scorpion appeared.

And the first scorpion scuttled right onto Alejandro's head.

"Get it off! Get it off!" he screamed.

"Uh-oh," Dora said, observing the two scorpions. "Another male. They will now fight."

And with that, the second scorpion leaped onto Alejandro's head.

"I'm not sure those guys are fighting," Randy said, eyeing them both.

"You're right, Randy!" Dora said. "It's a female. You can tell by the markings. They are not fighting. They are mating!"

It looked like Alejandro was about to explode, and his whole body went through a series of panicked convulsions at Dora's words. But he couldn't really move at all, just sort of vibrate in place.

"No, Alejandro! Stay still! Stay still!" Dora warned.

But it was already too late. Alejandro went under the quicksand, disappearing from view entirely. The scorpions were now resting on the surface of the mud. They paused for a moment, then scuttled away. The group looked at the spot where Alejandro had been and noticed a few bubbles popping on the surface.

Then nothing.

Randy didn't know what to do, so he turned away. Diego put his arm around Sammy, who leaned into him, holding the animal expert tightly.

Dora wasn't having it.

"No!" she said. "We have to do something! We can save him! Come on!"

As they were all about to follow Dora's lead, Randy

noticed something he hadn't seen just a second before. He pointed to a lower level, beneath the point where they were situated. There was an earthen outcropping. And there was something curious sticking out from the outcropping.

"I see . . . feet! Feet!" Randy hollered.

And it was feet! Specifically, it was Alejandro's feet, sticking out through the mud on the lower level!

Without time to spare, the kids hopped down to the lower level and grabbed hold of Alejandro's feet.

"Pull!" Diego shouted.

Alejandro slowly started to move.

"Pull harder!" Dora thundered.

Then all at once, Alejandro slipped free from the mud and tumbled to the ground. He was covered from top to bottom in thick mud. Sitting up, he looked at his young friends in complete and total disbelief.

"I'm alive?" he said, not quite believing it. "I'm alive? I'M ALIVE!"

Alejandro was laughing now, and then he started to cry. The kids all decided that it was kind of uncomfortable, watching him do both like that.

"It's so awkward when adults cry," Randy said. "You just don't know where to look."

Alejandro was still crying, but he was clearly happy. "I'm so sorry! My whole life is a lie! I'm a fraud!" Alejandro said.

"No, you're not," Dora said. "Everyone thinks that sometimes, Alejandro!"

Still crying, Alejandro said, "I'm a bad guy."

Dora reassured him. "No, no. You're not a bad guy. No one is, deep down inside."

At last, Alejandro stopped crying and took Dora's hand. Then he blew his nose with his handkerchief.

"Thank you, Dora," he said. "Thank you."

Then he looked around and didn't recognize where they were.

"Where are we?" he asked.

On the lower level, they could see a fire that was still smoldering, as well as sleeping gear—a bedroll, some blankets. There was even meat hanging from some racks.

"Someone lives here," Randy said ominously.

As if in response, they saw a shadow appear in a nearby corridor, and it looked like it was holding something—was it a weapon? The shadow was coming closer, closer, closer . . .

"And that someone's coming!" Alejandro said.

The group immediately huddled together, expecting the worst. The shadow came closer and closer, until it stepped into the room.

There was no fierce warrior or mercenary, but an old woman with a kind expression on her face. The "weapon" that they had noticed before was actually a gourd. The old woman dipped the gourd into a small pool of water and offered it to the group, smiling.

CHAPTER 16

"SHE HASN'T SEEN MY parents,"
Dora said, motioning toward the old woman
seated around the campfire. Dora and her companions were
inside the woman's modest home in the ruins, wiping mud
off themselves while sipping cups of warm tea.

"And . . . she doesn't seem very interested in helping me
find them," Dora finished.

Alejandro furrowed his brow. "Too bad," he said. "But
perhaps she knows how to get to Parapata . . ."

Suddenly, the old woman sat up, a fire blazing in her eyes.
"Parapata!" she exclaimed. Then she reached into a pouch,
grabbed a handful of something, and threw it on the fire.
Flames shot up from the campfire, reaching up to the ceiling! It would have burned their eyebrows off if they hadn't
fallen back.

"She seemed pretty interested in that," Sammy said.

After the flames subsided, the old woman shook her head
and reached inside the pouch once more. This time, she
pulled out what looked like several small ceramic figures. She
set them on the ground in front of the group.

"Are they supposed to be us?" Diego wondered, unsure.

The old woman said nothing, merely sat there, stone-
faced. Then she picked up a large rock and, in one swift

motion, smashed the little ceramic figures to pieces. Then she raised the rock once more and smashed those pieces into even smaller pieces.

"That seemed bad, right?" Randy asked, knowing the answer already. "Everyone thinks that was bad?"

Nobody said a word as the old woman started to speak. It was an ancient language, and no one in the group understood it.

No one, that is, except for Dora.

"What? What did she say?" Sammy asked.

"She said anyone seeking Parapata is cursed," Dora replied. Then, upon seeing the horrified looks on everyone's faces, she quickly followed up with, "But she also said she knows how to get you guys back downriver. She can take you home. All of you."

"But what about you?" Diego asked.

"My parents are in danger," Dora said. "I have to keep going, no matter what."

The old woman turned to face Dora, glaring at the teenager. There was a long silence.

It was broken by Randy as he exclaimed, "Yes! Yes! I'm saved! I mean, only if you're cool without us, obviously, D. You're cool, right? I can call you D, right?"

Dora smiled at Randy, nodding. Then she looked at Sammy.

"You got me into this mess," Sammy said. "But I guess you're getting me out of it now. So we'll call it even."

Diego turned to face Dora and sighed heavily. "I'm

coming with you," he said. "You're my cousin. I can't let you go alone. There's, like, rules about that."

Dora brightened.

"I'm coming," Alejandro jumped in. "We're a team, Dora."

"We'll continue east," she said. "I'm still confident my parents came this way."

"All right, Dora, Diego, let's head out. Can't lose any more time," Alejandro urged.

A short while later, the group had left the old woman's home and were back out on the jungle trail. She had led the companions to a fork in the road just outside of the ruins of the opera house. On one path, heading east, were Dora, Diego, and Alejandro. And on the other were Randy and Sammy, with the old woman acting as their guide.

"You have enough supplies for a few days," Dora said, sadness in her voice. "That should be enough."

Then Dora grabbed Randy, pulled him close, and gave him a ginormous hug. Randy froze for a moment, then hugged back.

"Take care of yourself," Randy whispered to Dora.

"Little trouble breathing," Dora said.

Randy instantly realized he was hugging Dora way too hard, to the point where he might actually be causing damage to her vital organs. He let go, embarrassed.

Then Diego approached Sammy, and the two looked at each other, smiling, awkward.

"I hope you don't die or anything," Sammy said. It was one of the nicest things she had ever said to anyone.

"Thanks," Diego replied. "You, too."

Diego raised his hand for a fist bump, figuring it was better to go with a standard goodbye like that. Sammy surprised him by pulling Diego in for a hug.

"Is she staring at us?" Sammy said, noticing Dora hovering nearby.

"Yup," Diego said.

"Okay, time to go," Sammy said, and the two groups parted ways.

Alejandro looked at Dora, and said, "Lead the way."

But before Dora could take so much as a step, the old woman spoke to her in Quechua.

"She says to stick to the path," Dora translated, and watched as the old woman walked off into the jungle with her friends.

❀ ❀ ❀

"Ugh, the air is so . . . thick!" Diego said.

The sun was going down once more, and Diego, Dora, and Alejandro had been walking through the jungle for most of the day. The path they had taken—and from which they hadn't deviated—had forced them to go through some particularly unforgiving terrain. They were covered in little cuts from thorns, and their limbs were tired and sore from hacking away at the brush to forge their way ahead.

"Are you sure we're not lost?" Alejandro asked. "It's been a while since the last marker."

It was true. They hadn't seen one of the signature red *O* markers in quite some time. But Dora hadn't lost faith.

"I'm sure there will be another marker just up ahead," she said, trying to sound upbeat.

Alejandro looked at Diego. They weren't so sure.

❊ ❊ ❊

The old woman was speaking to them in Quechua. Without Dora there to translate, Randy and Sammy had little to no clue exactly what she was saying to them. They had been walking all afternoon, and the sun was going down. They had followed the river, and had been running behind the old woman the entire time.

She was very nimble for someone her age. She seemed to know every nook and cranny of the jungle and was hopping and jumping at an ever-tightening pace.

"Why is she in such a hurry to get us out of here?" Randy wondered. "What's the rush?"

They kept on the path until they came to a point where it met the river directly. Sammy noticed there was a carved-out log floating right by the bank that looked like a canoe.

"And that is our way out of this nightmare," Sammy said, pointing at the canoe.

The old woman made a gesture with her arms for both kids to get into the canoe. As she raised her arms, Sammy thought she saw a tattoo.

It looked an awful lot like an Inca sun symbol.

Randy was just about to climb aboard the canoe when Sammy cried out, "Randy! Wait. Stop!"

Then Sammy grabbed Randy by the hand and pulled him behind her as they sprinted off into the jungle.

❀ ❀ ❀

"Not something you see every day," Diego said.

He was right. The trio had just come over a crest in the jungle and seen a truly unexpected sight. Stretching out before them was a large field full of giant red flowers. It was beautiful to behold.

As they approached the flowers, Diego was stunned by how tall they were. They were almost like trees!

"Nobody touch anything," Dora said.

Alejandro took Dora at her word. He walked very carefully as he tried to negotiate his way between two huge flowers. One step at a time. It was a nail-biting moment, as it looked like Alejandro might accidentally bump into the flowers at any second.

At last, he made it through unscathed. "Yes! Made it!" Alejandro shouted, pumping both arms in the air in victory.

Hitting the flower directly above him.

The plant reacted instantly, suddenly going into full bloom. The petals unfolded and touched those of another plant. That plant's petals in turn opened, touching those of another plant, and so on, and so on.

"Sorry," Alejandro said.

As far as their eyes could see, the plants were opening up across the field. Alejandro couldn't contain his curiosity, and bent over to look directly at one of the flowers.

Suddenly, a puff of spores exploded from the flower, right into Alejandro's face!

"Don't breathe it in!" Diego warned.

Then spores burst forth from plants all around the companions. The air was filled with tiny particles, small, airborne warriors looking to invade. Everyone covered their mouths.

"We're in a spore field!" Dora yelled.

"Well, let's get out of it!" Alejandro suggested.

It was a good suggestion.

They moved as fast as they could, as the spores whisked above their heads, raining down upon them.

"It's okay," Dora said. "If these were poisonous spores, we'd be dead by now . . ."

OKAY. THIS IS WHERE THINGS GET WEIRD, PEOPLE.

Dora looked at her cousin, only to see that he didn't look exactly 100 percent like himself. He looked more like a cartoon.

"What?" animated Diego said to Dora.

"Oh boy," Dora replied.

"What?" Diego asked, looking down at himself. And then he saw the same thing Dora saw. "Ahhhhhhh!"

"What's happening?" Alejandro asked.

Suddenly, the effect of the spores became apparent. They messed with everyone's perception, and made it seem like they were all a part of a 2-D cartoon. Even the jungle around them appeared to be animated!

"Sana sana colita de rana! Si no sana hoy, sanara mañana!"

Alejandro cried out joyously. "I'm a bug! I'm a bug! I don't need these clothes!"

And then he stripped off his clothes, completely freaking out, running through the jungle.

"I'm sure this will pass," Dora said. "It's fine."

"Fine?" Diego said. "Are you kidding me? This is incredible!"

Diego grabbed a vine and started to swing through the cartoon jungle, whooping all the way.

AND THEN THINGS GOT WEIRDER.

Because that's when a cartoon Boots landed right in front of Dora and said, "Hi there, Dora!"

"Boots!" Dora exclaimed. "You can talk!"

"I have always been able to talk," Boots replied proudly.

"Hi, Dora!"

It was Dora's map talking now!

"Hi there, Map!" Dora said, smiling. "I thought I lost you!"

"You could never lose me," said Map. "I'm always with you! I'm everywhere you go!"

"Hi, Dora!"

It was Dora's backpack! Who you'll recall has its own song, which we're not going to sing right now!

"And Backpack?" Dora asked, incredulous.

"My mouth is a zipper!" Backpack said. And do you know what? IT WAS!

"Everyone is here!" Dora said cheerfully.

And then a small rock said, "Hi, Dora!"

"I don't know you, small rock, but it is nice to make your acquaintance!" Dora said.

"Where should we go?" Boots asked, looking around the cartoon jungle.

"To Parapata!" Dora announced.

"Follow me, Dora!" said Map.

Then Dora raced into the jungle following Map, as Diego swung right beside her on a vine.

"It's just like our childhood, Dora!" Diego observed. "Look, I even found my baby jaguar!"

The pair continued into the jungle, as the now-shirtless Alejandro ran behind them, apparently still thinking he was a bug or something.

After a while, Dora reached a ravine, which suddenly seemed to be enveloped in a thick mist. On the opposite side of the ravine, she could see what looked like a book—her father's journal!

"Papi's journal!" Dora said. "They're nearby!"

"Just jump across, Dora!" Boots said with confidence.

Dora took a step back, then another, and started to run right for the edge of the ravine! She took a flying jump, and do you know what?

She fell!

Except the weird part was, when she fell, she got up and saw that she was right back on the edge of the ravine, where she'd started. Only now, the other side of the ravine seemed to be even farther away!

"Try again, Dora," Boots urged.

"I can't," Dora said. "I'm not ready."

"Try," the monkey said. "You'll see."

Dora decided she had nothing to lose by trying again. She took a few more steps back, got a running start, jumped, and . . .

. . . fell again.

But this time, instead of hitting the bottom, she was surprised to find herself caught in the arms of a cartoon Randy and a cartoon Sammy! They picked her right up and carried her over to the other side of the ravine.

"Where are we going?" Diego asked.

"Parapata!" Dora answered.

"Don't forget us, Dora!" said Map. "We'll always be there for you!"

Then Backpack said, "My straps are my arms!"

Which was true, if not especially relevant.

Then they headed off into the clouds, and we promise things will get a little less weird from this point on.

CHAPTER 17

"WHAT DO WE DO?"

"We should sing her a song. She likes songs. It'll make her feel better."

"What song?"

"Dragging our friends through the jungle
The dragging song
They almost died
The dragging song . . ."

"Oh, I'm not very good at this."

"It worked! She's waking up!"

❋ ❋ ❋

Suddenly, Dora awoke to find Randy staring directly into her face. She had a screaming headache but was excited to see that Randy didn't look like a cartoon anymore.

"Randy?" she asked tentatively, not sure if she could trust her senses.

"She's waking up!" Randy said.

Dora noticed that Randy and Sammy had dragged her, Diego, and Alejandro out from the field of weird flowers.

"You saved us," Diego said, amazed. "You came back."

"The old woman had the same tattoo as that curse symbol we've seen everywhere," Sammy said, a shudder running up and down her spine.

 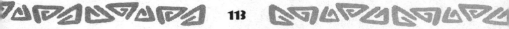

"Thank you so much, Sammy," Dora said gratefully. "I knew I could count on you!"

Sammy was a little embarrassed. "I just knew you guys were in danger," she said, trying to downplay her heroic act.

"By the way," Dora said, "not everyone at school hates you. I like you a lot."

Then Dora held Sammy's hand, and the two smiled.

"You like everyone a lot," Sammy replied. "Just rest. You're going to be okay."

Sammy and Randy finished dragging the three to a clearing, and then everyone collapsed on the ground and fell quickly asleep.

❀ ❀ ❀

"What happened back there?" Diego asked, sitting next to the campfire a few hours later. He was finally awake, and saw Dora sitting next to the fire, tending it. Behind them, Randy, Sammy, and Alejandro were asleep.

"I think it was a vision quest," Dora said. "I saw a mountain that moved every time I tried to jump. I knew I had to climb it, though. To get to Parapata. What did you see?"

Diego thought for a moment. "Memories," he started. "Of playing in the jungle with Boots and all the other animals. Of us as little kids."

Then he rested a hand on Dora's shoulder.

"I never forgot the jungle, Dora," he said. "I just hid that part of me from the world. It's not cool to admit one of your best friends growing up was a monkey. But it's true. And

you, Dora . . . You were my best friend. The first friend I ever had."

Dora reached out and took her cousin's hand. Diego smiled.

"I'm glad I came with you," he continued. "*This*, this is our next adventure, *prima*."

"Our next adventure, *primo*," Dora answered.

Dora noticed that someone behind them was stirring and turned to see Alejandro holding his head, wincing, and walking toward them.

"Ugh," he said, shaking his head. "I had the weirdest dream. I was running around a field going crazy, and I tore my shirt off."

"That wasn't a dream," Sammy said, now awake. "That's what actually happened."

"And you're not wearing a shirt," Dora pointed out.

Alejandro looked down to see that Dora was exactly right. "Oh yeah. Wow. Um, excuse me," Alejandro said, red in the face. "I need to find my shirt . . ."

✿ ✿ ✿

After some more sleep, the sun finally came up, and the group was about as well rested as they were going to be. Dora was studying her father's journal, staring at a sketch of a tall mountain surrounded by clouds.

Then Dora lowered the book, revealing that they were standing in front of the exact same mountain right now.

"Thank you, vision quest," Dora said, smiling.

As the group gathered up their belongings, Dora turned

to her friends. "We're on the right path!" she announced. "I know how to get to Parapata!"

Then she turned to face Randy and Sammy. "Are you sure you're ready for this?" she asked.

"Look, we've made it this far," Sammy said, determined. "I want to see it through. Together."

"Samesies," Randy added. "Let's finish this thing."

And with that, the companions were back on the jungle trail.

The trail leading up the mountain was narrow and treacherous, to say the least. The companions had to hug tight to the rock wall, as one wrong step could easily send them tumbling back down. As they advanced, they noticed the clouds began to drift in, blocking their view of where the trail ended and the sky began.

"The entrance to Parapata should be at the base of those mountains," she said, pointing into the distance.

"Nothing can stop us now!" Randy cheered.

Dora was just about to take another step forward into the fog, when a gust of wind blew it away—revealing that Dora was about to take a step into thin air. Alejandro's arm reached out like lightning and snatched Dora back from certain doom.

"Whew, that was close," Dora said, smiling at Alejandro.

Alejandro turned around and started to head up the hill. On his second step, the ground beneath him collapsed! Then the entire area around them collapsed, swallowing up Alejandro and the kids!

Boots managed to jump clear, but there was nothing he could do for Dora and her companions, except watch the calamity unfold.

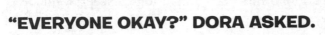

CHAPTER 18

"EVERYONE OKAY?" DORA ASKED.

She looked up and saw that they had fallen into a large cavern. Dust and debris wafted around them from above. It was dark, so Dora reached into her backpack and rummaged around for her flashlight. She found it and turned it on with a loud click.

Inside the illuminated cavern, Dora could see that they were surrounded by monkey statues. So many monkey statues.

All the monkey statues.

"Whoa," Diego said, which was a definite understatement. "This was all hidden down here?"

"Of course it was," Alejandro said, as if he knew about it all along. "And I knew that. So I did exactly what I did. Totally on purpose."

"Cool," Sammy said, unmoved. "Now we're stuck in a hole."

Dora looked up to the opening, which was high above them. There was no way they could jump to reach it, or climb.

Suddenly, Boots popped his little monkey head into the opening and chattered something to Dora.

"Boots!" she said. "We're okay. Go and see if you can find a way around!"

While looking up at Boots, Dora noticed that the ceiling

of the cave was covered in what looked like a giant painting of some kind. It looked like a blanket of gold and silver stars.

"Stars," Diego said.

"It's a star map," Dora and Randy said in unison.

"Classic us," Randy added.

But Dora didn't notice. "The stars aren't in the correct place," Dora said.

"Awesome!" Randy chimed in. "A jungle puzzle! And if we solve the jungle puzzle, we'll find Parapata!"

Alejandro approached Randy, shaking his head slightly. "I don't think this is a jungle puzzle. Mainly because there is no such thing as a jungle puzzle," Alejandro said.

Randy wasn't having it. "No way," he said. "I've seen several movies about the jungle. To solve this, we have to get the stars in the right position, and then some big stone wheels will turn and a treasure will be revealed. It's gonna be awesome. We just need to find a lever to pull. Like this one!"

Then Randy leaned over and pulled what looked like a lever on one side of the cavern. It must have been a lever, too, because as soon as Randy pulled it, there was a low, ominous rumbling sound.

"What is that?" Diego asked, worried.

"That does not sound like a good noise," Alejandro agreed.

"Oh, wait!" Dora said. "The stars *are* in the right position. It's the Southern Hemisphere. I was looking the wrong way around!"

"But it's still a jungle puzzle, right?" Randy said, because he really, really wanted to solve a jungle puzzle.

IF YOU REALLY WANT TO SOLVE A JUNGLE PUZZLE, TOO, THEN SAY, "JUNGLE PUZZLE!"

GO ON, WE'LL WAIT.

Before anyone could do anything else, water started to spray from an enormous stone faucet in the cavern.

"Wow!" Dora said. "This isn't a jungle puzzle at all . . . We're in a *puquio*!"

"What the flip is a *puquio*?" Sammy asked.

"It's an ancient underground aqueduct," Diego explained. "Inca engineers built some of the most elaborate irrigation systems ever devised. Water, from above, using gravity."

"The aqueducts allowed the Inca to thrive within the harsh jungle," Dora added.

This was all great and very informative, except for the fact that the water was now pouring into the room at quite a rapid rate, and it was actually filling it up. Feeling somewhat responsible on account of it was he who had pulled the lever in the first place, Randy returned to the lever and tried to yank on it to make it stop.

It didn't so much stop as it caused yet a second stone faucet to erupt with water, which knocked Dora right off her feet.

"Stop pulling levers!" Alejandro roared.

"I thought it was an off switch!" Randy shot back.

The water was rising, and the group was now swimming, trying to stay afloat, as the water continued to rush in unabated.

"If we're in an aqueduct, we have to somehow open the sluice gate!" Diego said.

"How do you know so much about aqueducts?" Sammy inquired.

"I really liked Inca stuff as a little kid," Diego said, treading water. "I kept all my books on Inca culture and architecture."

Diego glanced over at his cousin, who gave him a solid nod of approval.

"Now where is the sluice gate?" Diego wondered. "We just need to find the sluice gate!"

"Please stop saying 'sluice gate,'" Sammy asked.

Randy had a thought and dipped his head below the surface of the water. A couple of seconds later, he was back. "Does it look kinda like a big plug?" Randy said.

"Very possibly," Dora replied.

Then, following Randy's lead, everyone took a deep breath and ducked their heads beneath the water. Diego looked, and pointed at a wheel on the wall. When they all resurfaced, he said, "That must be the mechanism that opens the sluice gate."

As soon as the words "sluice gate" were out of his mouth, he felt Sammy staring at him with laser-beam intensity.

"It's what it's called!" he said defensively. "We have bigger things to deal with right now! Now give me a hand; it's going to take all of us!"

Taking another series of deep breaths, the companions ducked beneath the surface of the water and headed for the wheel. They grabbed it and started to pull.

But it wouldn't budge.

One by one, they popped up from the water, until everyone was there.

"You guys okay?" Dora asked, worried. The water was reaching the ceiling now. "We have one more chance at this. It's now or never. We can do this!"

"No!" Randy said. "I can do this!"

"I don't want to doubt you, Randy, but didn't you tell me you used to drown a lot at the public pool?"

"No, Dora," Randy said. "I used to *pretend* to drown. Who here can hold their breath for seven minutes? It's hard to tell with all this water, but I'm assuming none of you have your hands raised."

He'd assumed correctly.

"This one's mine," Randy said heroically.

Everyone realized that Randy was right. Time was running out, and he was their last, best hope. Taking a series of deep breaths, Randy took one final gulp of air, then disappeared under the water.

Swimming down, he grabbed the wheel and pulled again. It still wouldn't move. But Randy wasn't done. He kept on pulling, yanking the wheel as hard as he could.

Slowly, very slowly, it budged.

Just a little.

So Randy tugged some more.

And more.

The wheel slowly started to turn. Randy's muscles were burning from the effort, but he couldn't stop. He kept on

yanking on the wheel, until the giant plug—the one he'd noticed the first time he dunked his head under water—began to move out of the way.

The water began to run through the hole like a giant drain.

It happened so fast that all the water seemed to disappear through it at once, taking Dora, Diego, Sammy, Alejandro, and Randy right with it!

CHAPTER 19

AS IF THE PAST days hadn't been weird enough, now Dora and her friends found themselves swirling down the drain of some giant, ancient sink!

After she went down the stone pipe, Dora splashed right out and into a waterfall. Surrounded by foaming water, Dora thrust her arms and legs out as if trying to swim, or maintain her balance, or prevent herself from falling farther—or some strange combination of all those things.

She ended up falling down into a deep pool of water in a clearing. Roughly pulling herself ashore, Dora collapsed in a heap in the jungle dirt. Looking up, the sun was in her eyes, but she could have sworn someone was standing over her.

"Dora? Dora?!"

Dora couldn't see the face, but she recognized the voice.

"Mami?"

"Dora? But what—"

"Papi!" cried Dora, and jumped up from the dirt to find her mother and father, alive! Dora threw her arms around them both, and she hugged them harder than she'd ever hugged anyone before, probably even harder than Randy had hugged her the other day, when Dora thought she might have sustained minor spinal damage.

"My baby!" Elena swooned. "Oh, my baby! What are you doing here? What is going on?"

"You have no idea how happy I am to see you both!" Dora said, near tears. "I was so worried!"

Cole smiled at his daughter, beaming with pride. "I'm so happy to see you, too, but so confused," Cole said. "How did you find us? What were you doing in the *puquio*?"

Suddenly, there was another splash in the water, and a moment later, Diego's head popped up from the pool.

"Randy did it!" Diego cried, pulling himself up. "We're alive!"

"Diego?" Elena said.

"Tía! Tío!" Diego answered.

Cole looked dumbfounded. "How is this possible? Please, will someone explain what is happening."

Dora smiled. "It's a long story," she said. "We were kidnapped by mercenaries in search of Parapata, but we—"

"Kidnapped?" Elena said, horrified. "Are you okay?! Did they hurt you?!"

"Who kidnapped you?" Cole asked, his voice full of fatherly concern. "Where are they?"

SPLASH!

This time, it was Randy's turn to appear.

"Okay, that was epic!" he said. "I did something epic. I'm basically a superhero." Suddenly, Randy realized he wasn't all alone and was standing next to two people who could only be Dora's parents. "Oh, hi, Mr. and Mrs. Dora," he said.

SPLASH!

That was Sammy.

"Super annoyed my teachers skipped aqueducts. That's

 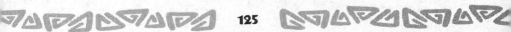

just negligent," she said, then she noticed Dora's parents as well. "Hello, Dora's parents."

"Are you still in danger?" Cole asked.

That wasn't the only question in the air. "Who are all these people?" Elena inquired.

"We're Dora's friends from school!" Sammy interjected. Sammy, Randy, and Diego stood shoulder to shoulder with Dora, looking like a well-oiled team.

"Yep," said Randy. "And this is one crazy field trip."

"These mercenaries," Cole pondered out loud, "who are they?"

"It's okay," Dora said, trying to reassure her father. "Alejandro saved us from them at the airport. He's here with us!"

SPLASH!

Right on cue, Alejandro dropped into the pool.

"Who?" Elena asked.

"Your old friend Alejandro," Dora said, with a "duh" kind of look on her face. "From the university! You sent him your journal . . ."

Alejandro pulled himself up just like all the others and stood up on the shore of the pool.

"Are you okay, Alejandro?" said Dora.

Alejandro looked at Dora, then smiled. Except the smile kept on going, and the edges of his mouth curled, to the point where it looked . . . cruel, somehow. Then he pulled a plastic bag from his pack, revealing a walkie-talkie.

"Bravo team," Alejandro said into the walkie-talkie, "this is Alpha leader."

Dora looked at her very confused parents, feeling more than a little confused herself. "You . . . don't . . . know . . . him, do you?" Dora said, the situation now dawning on her. "Oh *mier . . . coles . . .*"

"We found them," Alejandro said, glaring at Dora's parents. "Delta rendezvous point. You have my location."

Cole looked at Alejandro with disdain. "I've never seen this man in my life. And my journal was stolen days before we left on our expedition!" he said.

Heartbroken, Dora spun around to face Alejandro. "You lied to me," she said, unable to believe that someone could be so evil.

"No," Alejandro said, correcting the teenager, "I outwitted you. As I have outwitted every adversary that came before you. The greatest investigative minds of the century have failed to thwart my heists. The crown jewels of the Ivory Coast . . . the Comtesse de Vendôme necklace . . . and now the gold of Parapata."

He took a step, and then another, walking around Dora as he spoke. "Who would have believed that my greatest achievement . . . the final act in a prosperous treasure-hunting career . . . would find me squaring off against a socially inept jungle nerd and three high school losers. I almost wish you had made it more of a challenge," Alejandro said, taunting Dora.

As he finished his rant, Dora saw Viper, Christine X, and Powell—the three mercenaries—splash down into the pool. They rose up, then quickly encircled Dora and her companions. Alejandro stepped forward, taking his place as their leader.

"Who are you, and what do you want with my daughter?" Cole demanded.

"You've raised quite a remarkable girl, Professors Marquez," Alejandro said. "Smart, trusting, and yet . . . so, so dumb."

That was about all Cole was willing to listen to. He leaped for Alejandro, ready to attack, but was caught at the last second by the other mercenaries. They held him back, while Alejandro got right in Cole's face.

"Now, if you please, you will lead me to Parapata," Alejandro said. The words were polite, but the tone and meaning were anything but.

"Impossible," Elena countered. "We don't even know where it is!"

Alejandro looked at Elena, wrinkling his nose and smiling. "I don't believe you," he said. "You've been ahead of us for weeks. You've set up camp. My guess is, you've found Parapata . . . and it's nearby. Yes?"

Neither Cole nor Elena did anything to deny it.

"You'll never get inside," Cole said. "It's impenetrable."

"As your daughter is so fond of saying, if you just believe in yourself, anything's possible," Alejandro teased. "You wouldn't want anything to happen to her, now, would you?"

"No," Cole said through gritted teeth.

"Good!" Alejandro answered. "If everyone just plays nice, I'll get my gold and you'll be on your way home, safe and sound. You're a smart family, right? So make the smart choice."

Dora knew there was no choice at all.

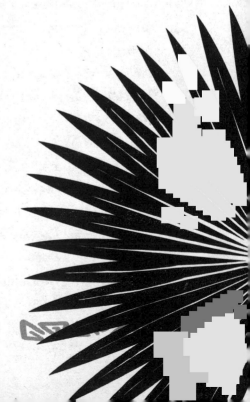

CHAPTER 20

IT DIDN'T ALWAYS RAIN in the jungle, but it was certainly starting to seem that way.

Only a couple of hours had passed since Alejandro had revealed himself to be the leader of the desperate, cutthroat band of mercenaries that had kidnapped Dora and her friends and brought her to the jungle in search of a city of lost gold.

Now they were back on the jungle trail, hiking along a narrow path. Alejandro was right beside Dora's mom, with Dora's dad behind them, face buried in his journal. Behind them were the kids, each of whom had their hands tied, making their escape next to impossible. And behind them was Viper.

"I'm so sorry," Dora said to her cousin. "This is all my fault."

"It's okay," Diego said quietly.

"It's not okay," Dora said. "Alejandro's right. I'm so dumb. So, so dumb."

"You're not dumb," Diego said. "You just trust people. You expect them to be good. We should all be more like you."

The wind had definitely left Dora's sails. "I thought believing in yourself was enough," she said despondently, "but it isn't."

"Well, to actually be able to succeed at something usually requires hours and hours of practice," Diego replied.

"And some actual talent," Randy added.

"Sometimes your parents have to know a friend who knows a friend," Sammy offered.

"Timing is also an important factor," said Randy.

"And luck can play a big part, too," said Diego.

"The important thing is that you're safe," Cole said, turning his head toward the kids. "We're safe. If we just do what he says, we'll be fine."

"But he is stealing the greatest treasure right out from under you!" Dora protested.

"Dora, you're our most important treasure," Elena said. "We would protect you over anything. It's why we didn't want you to come."

"I'm sorry," Dora said. "I'm so, so sorry . . ."

Alejandro had heard about enough at this point, and looked like he was ready to leap out of his skin. "Can you all shut up back there?" he ordered. "I've had to listen to your BS for three days. Your relentless good-natured spirit is a holy nightmare. So just shut up. Shut up!"

Dora couldn't help herself, and started to speak.

"Shhhhhhhut up! No more talking!" Alejandro said, and the look on his face said that he wasn't kidding around. "And definitely no more singing!"

Dora was bummed about no more singing.

A while later, the rain started to clear, and the sun began to poke its way through the thick cloud cover above. As Dora trudged along the path, she winced as the ropes that bound

her wrists chafed and rubbed the skin raw. She'd lost all track of time at this point and had consigned herself to following Alejandro in the hope that maybe she and her friends and family might escape this situation with their lives.

Walking along, Dora saw something moving overhead—a shadow. It darted quickly, in and out of the branches, and Dora craned her neck upward to try to get a glimpse of whatever it was.

Boots! It was Boots!

She saw the monkey up in the trees, tracking the kids along the jungle path.

Maybe there would be a way to save the day yet . . . !

Up ahead, Dora saw that Cole and Elena had led the group to a large rock edifice. As they rested for a moment, Cole said, "Parapata is a find of global significance."

"Why have you stopped here?" Alejandro demanded. "This is it . . . isn't it?"

Impatient, Alejandro shoved Cole aside and barged through the rest of the group as he walked through a hidden crevice. Everyone followed suit behind Alejandro. The crevice became more and more narrow as they shimmied through, and even Dora wondered if she might get stuck.

But no one did get stuck, and when they emerged from the crevice, Dora was stunned to see something in the mist, in the distance: a pair of enormous gates, tall, with sheer cliffs on either side.

The gates to Parapata.

"Parapata . . ." Dora said in awe.

"It's real," Diego said.

"And absolutely impenetrable," Cole finished.

Alejandro nudged Cole and Elena, making them walk forward. "We'll see about that! Powell, get the dynamite for the gate!"

"The what?" Elena said, her brain exploding. "Are you insane? It's a historic site!"

"I just want what I came for," Alejandro said, not making a big deal out of it. "The gold. Greedy, I know. Call me old-fashioned."

Cole couldn't believe what he was hearing. "Dynamite will bring the entire site crumbling in on itself!" he pointed out. "The Inca would rather bury their city than let it fall into the hands of conquerors and thieves!"

Alejandro considered that for about a half second. "Why do you think you and your wife are here?" he asked. "Now get me inside."

"We've already been here two weeks and have barely scratched the surface!" Elena said. "There's still so much to translate and work out!"

"And now you have until morning. Whether you're ready or not, we *will* enter Parapata."

Elena and Cole didn't say anything, knowing there was nothing they could do to change Alejandro's mind.

"Either by force or some sacrifice . . . on your part," Alejandro continued. "We make camp tonight by those gates."

 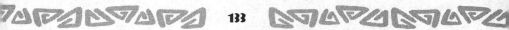

Reluctantly, Cole and Elena moved ahead to start setting up camp. Everyone followed in a single-file line.

Without warning, Boots suddenly descended from above, silently, right on top of Dora! Immediately, he started untying Dora's ropes, but she tried to shoo him away—if the mercenaries saw Boots now, who knew what they might do?

Suddenly, Viper whirled around, responding to the commotion. Dora was there, but Boots wasn't. She pretended that her hands were still tied. So far, Viper hadn't seemed to notice that they were, in fact, free. Then he heard . . . Was it whistling? Viper looked up, and saw a monkey hanging in the branches above, whistling.

Viper rolled his eyes, turned around, and headed to the campsite.

❊❊❊

As they continued their trek, Boots worked his magic one by one, untying Sammy, Diego, and Randy. Each time, he was almost caught in the act—either by Viper or by that weird, mask-wearing fox, Swiper.

But each time, Boots managed to evade detection, or to just appear like some regular, ordinary, jungle-variety monkey who was just hanging around, sticking his tongue out, making noises, and just generally being obnoxious.

After a while, Viper had enough of the monkey's shenanigans, and especially of all the commotion that was coming out of the kids.

"What's going on back here?" Viper asked, his patience evaporating by the second. "Let's go; we're lagging behind!"

That's when Randy accidentally dropped the untied ropes that he clutched in his hands to make Viper think he was still tied up. He hoped Viper wouldn't notice.

Viper noticed.

His eyes went wide as he realized what was going on.

Then Dora shouted, "Run!"

Like a shot, Diego, Sammy, and Randy took off into the jungle, disappearing into the lush greenery. But Dora stayed behind. Thrusting an arm into her backpack, she pulled out . . . her yo-yo.

Viper was just about to alert the other mercenaries, when Dora flicked the yo-yo out from her hand and smacked Viper right between the eyes! The mercenary then hit the ground, unconscious.

"It really is the deadliest weapon," Dora said proudly.

"Viper! What's going on?"

Dora recognized the voice. It was Powell, calling out for Viper. Deciding what her next move should be, Dora picked herself up and raced off into the jungle after her companions.

A few seconds later, Powell arrived and surveyed the scene before him. Viper, knocked out, on the ground. The kids, gone. Then Powell raised his gun and pointed it into the jungle.

"Put that down!" Alejandro ordered, running up to Powell. "What happened?"

"The girl escaped with her friends!" Powell said.

Alejandro stepped forward, looking out into the jungle, his face a twisted grimace. "I'll handle it," he said. "Take the professors to the gate. I spent three days with these brats; I know what they'll do next."

CHAPTER 21

DORA WAS RUNNING THROUGH
the jungle, faster than she ever had before. Leaping over logs, avoiding poisonous frogs, climbing over tree trunks—nothing was going to slow her down.

"Diego!" she shouted. "Sammy! Randy! Where are you guys?"

Then Dora did something she wasn't accustomed to.

She tripped.

She fell down hard and rolled into a gulley, landing among some old, gnarly tree roots. Dora was all alone in the jungle, until she realized that Boots had joined her and helped to pull her up into a sitting position.

Except Dora wasn't glad to see Boots.

Rather, it was the opposite.

"Boots! You shouldn't have done that!" Dora said, berating the poor little monkey. "I literally led the bad guy to my parents, and you just made it worse!"

Boots didn't say anything, because monkey.

"This is no time for taking risks!" Dora continued. "You've put everyone in danger!"

Boots said nothing again.

"You didn't save me!" she hollered. "Papi said to do whatever Alejandro asked!"

No, Boots did not say anything to that, in case you were wondering.

"So what if he's a double-crossing mercenary treasure hunter? Once my parents show him the treasure, he'll let us go!"

More Boots not talking.

"He's . . . not going to want anyone else to know where the treasure is," Dora said, and it slowly dawned on her. "Which means he's going to kill them, isn't he? He's going to kill all of us! Oh no. Oh no, oh no!"

Boots stared.

"But what can I do?" Dora asked. "My parents were right. I am too impulsive and trusting. It turns out, it doesn't matter if you believe in yourself—lots of stuff is impossible!"

Boots opened his mouth and said—JUST KIDDING. Boots is a monkey, can't talk, thought we already established that earlier in this chapter.

"I can't save them," Dora said. "Not by myself. I'm just a kid."

Boots looked at Dora and then said, "You're not a kid. But you're not a grown-up either, Dora. You're a teenager. It's a super-confusing time. But the fact is, you're right. You can't do it by yourself. The good news is, you have friends now. And together, anything is possible."

"Boots! You can talk!" Dora said, amazed.

You must be really amazed, considering we've been telling you all along that Boots can't talk, and yet here he was, just talking.

Except Boots had gone back to not talking now. He was quiet and picked a bug out of Dora's hair and ate it.

"Boots? Boots?" Dora begged.

But the monkey didn't say anything. Dora sighed and heard the sound of crunching leaves coming from behind. She spun around on her heels and saw Diego, Randy, and Sammy right there!

"Did you hear that?" Dora asked.

"You talking to a monkey? Yup," said Sammy.

"No, Boots talking to me!" Dora said.

"Maybe she hit her head," Randy mused.

"I'm fine," Dora said. "Come on, guys. Alejandro is never going to let us go. We have to save my parents!"

"How?" Diego asked, shrugging his shoulders. "They're armed mercenaries and we're teenagers."

"All Alejandro wants is gold. If we get inside Parapata, we can trade the treasure for my parents."

But Sammy wasn't convinced. "Alejandro can't be trusted," she said, and she was right. "He'll never let us leave here alive!"

Dora didn't disagree. "Alejandro has shown his true self," she said. "I know who he is now. When the time comes, I'll be ready for him."

"Fine, but your parents have been trying for weeks to get inside. How are we supposed to do any better?" Sammy asked.

"I don't know how we're going to get in, but I know we're

going to figure it out. Together," Dora said. "Tonight."

"Come. On!" Diego said. "How many times do I have to remind you that it's dangerous to explore the jungle at night?"

Dora looked at her cousin, and a smile crept up the corner of her mouth. "Tonight, *primo*, we break some rules."

CHAPTER 22

UNDER THE COVER OF darkness,
they approached. From her backpack, Dora had
snatched a pair of high-powered binoculars, and she had
Alejandro's campsite in view. She could make out her parents, sequestered in a tent (going over her father's journal, no doubt). Then there were the mercenaries. A sweep of the binoculars revealed Viper and Christina X standing guard by the tent.

Moving the binoculars along the ground, Dora zoomed over to the gates of Parapata. Standing in front, keeping watch, was Powell.

And Swiper.

"How do we get past him?" Diego asked.

Dora smiled. "Swiper."

A plan started to form in Dora's mind, and it was a doozy.

✿ ✿ ✿

Outside the gates to Parapata, Swiper paced back and forth on his little fox feet. Nothing was going to escape his notice.

Certainly not the bag that dropped from a nearby tree and onto the ground right near him. He absolutely noticed that. The curious fox couldn't help himself and trotted over to the bag. Swiper looked at it, sniffed it. Then he shook the bag with his teeth until it opened.

Something fell out.

Swiper howled.

"Whatcha got there?" Powell wondered, seeing the fox going nuts. He looked at the thing that fell out of the sack and saw a frog. A harmless little frog.

A harmless little bright yellow frog.

Powell reached down and picked it up. "It's just a little frog, buddy," Powell said, trying to calm Swiper's nerves. But as soon as Powell touched the frog, he fell over, his body completely frozen.

That's because it wasn't just any old frog—it was a golden poison frog. (If you were paying attention, you would remember that we talked about him earlier. We hope you were paying attention.)

Then the frog, doing what frogs do best, hopped, and hopped, and hopped, right onto Swiper's shoulder. One touch, and the fox fell down to the ground beside Powell, paralyzed as well.

The frog kept on hopping along.

Dora, Diego, Sammy, and Randy emerged from the darkness and ran up the stone steps toward the gate.

"There must be a way to open the gates from the outside," Dora whispered.

Looking around, Sammy saw a number of statues of different animals lining the walls. "Hey, guys," she said. "Look at these. Each one has a lever."

Sammy was right. There were about two dozen statues, each one of a different animal. And each one had a lever.

 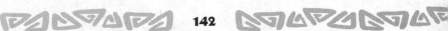

"I was wrong about jungle puzzles," Randy said. "There's no such thing as jungle puzzles." To prove his point, Randy reached out to one of the statues to pull a lever.

"Wait!" Dora hissed. "Don't do that!"

Dora pointed behind her to the hundreds of holes in the walls that surrounded them.

"Traps," she said. "Could be arrows. Or poison."

That gave Diego pause to think. He knelt down and jiggled one of the stone tiles upon which he was standing. "Looks like traps everywhere," he said. "This is some security system."

"How do we know which levers to pull?" Sammy wanted to know. "There's so many combinations!"

"Look for clues," Dora said quickly. "There have to be clues nearby."

"We're wasting time here, guys. You probably just need something boring, like a key or a battering ram," Randy said, clearly not feeling the whole "jungle puzzle" thing anymore.

The group split up, silently exploring the area, looking for anything that might possibly present itself as a clue.

"It's too dark to see anything!" Sammy called out.

"Correct," Diego said. "Hence the whole 'don't explore the jungle at night' thing!"

Dejected, Randy stared at the ground, when he noticed something strange seemed to be happening. One of the stone tiles seemed to glow, somehow turning a bit brighter, before the glow faded away.

"What the . . ." he said.

Then he looked up to the sky, and saw that the moon, which had been there just a moment ago, had disappeared behind some clouds. He waited for the clouds to pass and the moon to emerge. It did, and as the moonlight hit the ground, Randy was astounded.

All along the ground, hundreds of glittering mineral dots embedded in the stone tiles began to glow with reflected moonlight.

"Guys, look down!" Randy said excitedly.

The dots appeared to make random pictures.

No, wait. Not random pictures.

"They look like . . . constellations!" Dora and Randy said in unison. They looked at each other in amazement.

"Classic us, again," Randy said. "The same brain, in two very, very different bodies."

But again, Dora wasn't paying attention. She was focused on Diego, smiling. "Never explore the jungle at night?" she asked coyly.

They studied the constellation patterns on the ground. "It's Yasou Mayu," she said. "The Inca night sky. This one is Anca, the eagle. And Atoq, the fox."

"This one looks like a serpent. Are there any more?" Sammy asked.

"Here," Diego said. "This one's Otorongo, the jaguar. They're indigenous to this region. Apparently, I know that."

Instinctively, the kids each moved in front of an animal statue that corresponded with one of the constellations seen on the stone tiles beneath their feet.

"But what order do we pull them in?" Randy asked, gesturing toward a lever.

"Maybe we pull them all at once?" Diego theorized.

They looked at the traps all around them and realized that one wrong decision, one wrong move, and it was bye-bye, Dora and friends.

"That's a big 'maybe,'" Sammy said.

"On three, we pull," Dora decided. "Ready?"

"One," Randy said, gulping.

"Two," Sammy said, continuing the countdown.

"Three!" Diego finished, and the four kids each pulled their levers down.

And then, right before their very eyes, NOTHING HAPPENED.

"It's official," Randy said with a sigh. "Movies lie."

And then, right before their very eyes, SOMETHING HAPPENED.

The gates began to open.

"A jungle puzzle!" Randy said, suddenly excited. "A real freakin' jungle puzzle! So awesome! I'm sorry for doubting you, movies!"

CHAPTER 23

THE SIGHT THAT AWAITED Dora and her friends was truly glorious. Unlike the ruins they had encountered previously, the main street of Parapata looked as if it had been untouched by the unforgiving hand of time. The city sparkled all around them, with statues and terraces on all sides.

It was like magic.

"It's like they just left it, isn't it?" Sammy said, her mouth hanging open.

"I've never seen anything like it," Dora said, taking it all in. "This is the discovery of a lifetime. Do you realize how much we could learn about the Inca?"

Randy walked through the streets, and stared at a statue of a monkey. Then he saw another statue, this one of a horse wearing armor.

"A lot, I'm going to say a lot," Randy said. "Like, they really liked dressing up animals in human clothing. Look, this monkey's wearing boots."

That's because it *was* Boots. The monkey had scrambled in through the gates alongside Dora. She gave Boots a knowing look as the monkey scratched his chin.

"Whoa, weird," Dora said. They reached the end of the corridor, which led them directly to a temple. It appeared to be the centerpiece of the entire city.

"The temple," Diego said in awe.

"The gold, right?" Randy said. "This is totally where the gold is hidden."

"Everything the Inca treasured will be in here," Dora said. "But remember. We're explorers. Not treasure hunters."

Sammy stepped up. "We're not treasure hunters, but Alejandro is. So let's get there quickly. Come on—I don't do last!" she reminded them.

The quartet raced for the temple.

✤✤✤

The temple was pitch-black when they entered. Dora reached into her backpack and pulled out a box of strike-anywhere matches. Dragging one swiftly along the ground, she lit the match, then lit a torch that Diego had just finished preparing.

But instead of the torch revealing untold wonders, the temple itself appeared to be vacant.

"It's empty," Sammy said. "I don't get it."

"I don't see any doors," Diego said, looking around the large room.

"This can't be all there is," Dora said, thinking out loud.

"Dang, it was probably cleaned out by Spanish conquistadors," Diego mused.

"Yeah," Randy agreed. "Or the British."

"Or the French," Diego volunteered.

"Or the Americans and the United Fruit Company," Sammy added.

Walking around the empty temple, Randy came across a monkey statue in the corner. He leaned on it absentmindedly.

The statue tilted, and a bowl that had been in the monkey's hands slipped out. Randy caught the bowl with his own hands before it could hit the ground.

"I found this bowl!" Randy shouted. "Is it treasure?"

Dora ran over to Randy to examine the find. "That's . . . a sun bowl!" Dora said.

"Check it out," Diego said. "There's one in every corner!"

Looking around, Dora saw that Diego was correct. In each corner of the room, there was a nearly identical monkey statue. Each of the monkeys was holding a sun bowl in its paws.

"Oh, cool!" Randy said. "So what's a sun bowl do?"

"Don't look at me." Diego shrugged.

Now it was Sammy's turn to blindside everyone with some knowledge. "You tilt the bowls at a certain angle to reflect the sunlight," she said. "Look! There's an opening in the wall for the sun to shine in. But they're usually designed to only work during summer solstice."

"Well, we don't exactly have time to wait for the summer solstice," Randy said impatiently.

Dora smiled. "Which is why we have modern technology."

Then she reached into her amazing backpack—GO AHEAD, SING THE SONG IF YOU WANT—and pulled out her high-powered flashlight. She turned it on, then tossed it to Boots. The monkey scampered up the side of the temple, to the small hole in the wall that Sammy had mentioned. Boots then held the flashlight there, in the exact position the sun would be in, and illuminated the bowl that Randy held in his hands.

"Now what?" Randy asked.

"You have to angle the bowl to hit a certain point in the room," Dora advised.

"But to do that," Sammy said, working it out, "we have to figure out the correct angle."

Sammy and Dora looked at each other, and then started to look around the temple at the horizontal patterns on the walls. There were squares inscribed into the middles of circles. Then another square inside each square, at a ninety-degree angle. Sammy and Dora looked at them, tilting their heads.

Diego started to ask what they were doing, but Sammy quickly shushed him.

"Clearly they love geometry," Dora observed.

"Everything fits together symmetrically," Sammy said.

"Forty-five degrees!" they shouted together. Then they high-fived. Dora ran and grabbed one of the bowls, tilting it to a forty-five-degree angle. The flashlight hit the bowl, bouncing the beam of light toward Diego, who angled his bowl, reflecting the light to the third bowl in Randy's hands, who reflected it to Sammy, who held the fourth bowl. The final beam of light reflected onto a tile on the opposite wall. Nothing appeared; there was no huge magic reveal.

Until . . .

There was a loud rumbling sound, and a door appeared on the wall with the single illuminated tile. Then the door began to slide open!

"A door!" Diego shouted. "It's opening a door!"

The excitement grew as the door opened.

And opened.

And opened some more.

It was a big, heavy door, and it was taking forever to open, is what we're saying.

"Could it open a little faster?" Sammy asked.

"Yeah," Randy said. "My arms are getting tired!"

They were all still holding the bowls as the beam of light continued to shine on the spot on the wall, causing the door to open.

"Just hold the beam of light until it's open!" Dora called out.

Diego held the bowl in his hands as his eyes wandered over to the wall next to him. He looked at the ornate patterns on the walls and saw what looked to be renderings of the Ancient Inca, holding arms and leaping through the air.

"What is that?" Diego said. "Some kind of Ancient Inca group hug?"

This prompted Sammy to look at the patterns beside her, and she noticed there was the hollow eye socket of a carved skull. And then a spider slowly appeared from the eye socket!

Sammy gasped at the sight of the spider, accidentally dropping her bowl to the ground. The bowl smashed into several small, un-put-back-togetherable pieces.

With the beam of light broken, the door stopped opening. Everyone turned to look at Sammy.

"It slipped!" she said. "I'm sorry!"

Then there came another rumbling noise.

"Um, guys?" Randy said. "You might want to look up."

And when they looked up, they saw what Randy had just noticed.

The ceiling was descending. There were dark splotches on the ceiling, and it became clear those were the "leftovers" from previous intruders.

"We didn't hold the beam of light long enough!" Dora said.

"The jungle puzzles have turned on us!" Randy moaned.

"The door is closing!" Sammy pointed out.

"Everyone run!" Dora yelled.

CHAPTER 24

THE FOUR TEENAGERS SPRINTED

toward the rapidly closing door. It was ironic, considering how slowly the door had opened. It seemed to move disproportionately faster as it closed.

But it wasn't a great moment to appreciate irony.

Diego was first through the door, pulling Sammy through right behind him. Next was Randy, with Dora right behind him. As Randy made his way through the door, he looked around, only to find the passageway had become too narrow for Dora to pass through safely!

"Dora!" Randy screamed.

Dora reached her hand through and Randy grabbed it. He pulled on her arm but just couldn't seem to pull her in.

"Try and pull it open!" Diego said urgently.

Diego, Randy, and Sammy pulled with all their might on the door. They felt like they were going to pass out, but the door moved slightly.

"It's not enough!" Sammy said, and it wasn't.

But the ceiling had continued to descend, and Dora was still trapped in the room. And to make matters worse, spikes were now protruding from the ceiling, waiting to puncture the teenager with the nontalking monkey and the nontalking map and the nontalking backpack and . . . You get the picture.

But before Dora could be skewered, Boots jumped down from the ceiling and braced himself with his arms, legs, and tail between the closing stone door and the wall. Then he started to push, like a mighty monkey jack!

"That's it, Boots!" Dora cried.

The monkey's plan worked! The door had been pried open just enough for Dora to squeeze through. She barely made it to the others as the ceiling and spikes slammed to the floor. The door closed, and the teenagers and Boots collapsed on the floor in a heap.

✿✿✿

Having recovered from the debacle of the lowering ceiling of spikes and the slow-opening/fast-closing door, Dora and her companions were now making their way down a long corridor.

"Thank you, Boots," Dora said, giving Boots a scratch on the chin.

The four friends put their arms around one another and looked down the hallway.

"It goes on forever," Randy said.

"At the end," Sammy said, noticing something. "Is that . . ."

There was a room visible at the end. Even from here, the kids could see that the room was filled with a giant stone statue of a monkey.

"Look at that giant monkey!" Randy said. "We did it, guys! We found the treasure!"

"C'mon, Dora! This is it!" Diego added.

At once, Randy, Sammy, and Diego started to run down

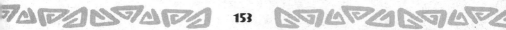

the corridor toward the room with the giant monkey statue. But something didn't seem quite right to Dora . . .

"Wait," Dora said. "Guys, this seems too—"

Just as Dora tried to issue her warning, the ground beneath the others let out a loud click. Randy, Sammy, and Diego looked down, only to find that they were standing on a large tile with a huge sun emblem upon it.

". . . easy," Dora said, finishing her thought.

"Oh, come on!" Sammy raged.

The next thing anyone knew, the entire corridor tilted downward, and everyone slid down the corridor like it was a giant amusement-park slide! The teenagers were racing down the corridor on their backs, momentum increasing, as they hurtled toward the room with the monkey statue.

Except as the angle changed, so too did their view— which was now replaced with a massive pit of sharpened spears! They couldn't help but notice there were bones lining the bottom of the pit, no doubt from previous interlopers who had come seeking the fabled lost treasure.

"Spears!" Randy screamed. That was the first time in his life he had ever made that exclamation, and the way things were going, it seemed like it would be the last.

With their arms around one another, the group continued to slide down the corridor, out of control.

It looked like this would be the end of their journey, and of their lives.

Then Diego spotted something on the wall—it was the same image of the Ancient Inca arm in arm, like the pattern

he had seen on the wall in the temple. They were leaping through the air, just like they were back in the temple, too. And that gave him an idea . . .

"At the very end of the corridor, everyone jump together!" Diego shouted.

"What? We'll never make it!" Randy hollered.

"It's too far!" Sammy protested.

"It's an illusion!" Diego said. "Trust me!"

The end came a lot faster than they would have liked, and they were just upon the pit of spears.

"Now! Jump!" Diego called.

They did exactly that, jumping off the end of the corridor, arm in arm, over the spear pit.

The group narrowly missed the spear pit, landing hard on the ground right next to it. They clung to one another tightly, rolled, and finally came to rest.

That's when they realized the corridor wasn't nearly as long as it had appeared to be.

"It was forced perspective!" Dora realized. "A trick to fool thieves and trespassers! Good job, Diego!"

Diego smiled at his cousin. "Ancient Inca group hug for the win."

The floor then slid back into place, and the spear pit was covered once more. Everything appeared just as it had before they had stepped on the sun tile, activating the trap.

Having reached the chamber with the monkey statue, the group surveyed the room. It was a large room that had no roof. There were vines everywhere, creeping and crawling

all over every available surface. There were rocks protruding from the walls, which were covered in vines as well.

As they walked around the room, they realized that the corridor trap wasn't the only thing that utilized forced perspective. Up close, the "giant" monkey statue was only about two feet tall!

"The monkey looked a lot more impressive back there," Randy noted.

The monkey's arms were outstretched, with a gurgling water fountain on either side of it. Resting before the monkey was a large altar. On the altar, there was a plethora of treasure, valuables of all kinds. Rubies, emeralds, gold. Armor, weapons, jewelry. It was the treasure of a lifetime, of several lifetimes.

"This looks pretty impressive to me," Sammy said, looking at the bounty before them.

"Is that an emerald?" Diego asked, eyeing one particular gem.

"It's bigger than a basketball," Sammy said.

"I'm thinking we found the treasure," Diego replied.

"No," Dora said. "This is the final puzzle."

There was writing below the monkey. It was in an ancient tongue that no one spoke anymore.

Except Dora.

Reading aloud, she said, "'Make an offering to the Gods of that which is most revered.'"

"There must be a hundred random offerings laid out here," Sammy said, looking at the vast assortment of treasure on the altar.

"That's the puzzle," Dora said. "We have to figure out which one to offer."

"So what did the Inca revere most?" Sammy asked.

Dora and Diego looked at one another, thinking.

"That's easy," came a voice from behind.

The teenagers spun around and saw him.

Alejandro.

CHAPTER 25

ALEJANDRO STOOD THERE AT
the entrance to the monkey chamber, having survived the corridor slide. Diego, Sammy, and Randy looked
surprised, shocked to see the mercenary.

Dora did not.

Alejandro smiled his wicked smile and seemed only too
happy to share what he thought the Inca revered more than
anything.

"The same as me," Alejandro said. "Gold."

"Ah, crud." Randy winced.

"Thanks for getting through the tough stuff for me,"
Alejandro said, nodding to Dora. "Once again, I only had to
follow Miss Know-It-All, and she led me straight to the gold.
Seriously, how can such a clever girl be so stupid?"

"Dora is not stupid," Sammy argued. "Sure, she acts stupid, she says stupid things, and she wears stupid clothes, but
if you're forced to spend time with her twenty-four/seven,
you'll find out she's really not."

"That's the sweetest thing anyone has ever said about me,"
Dora said with a smile. "Thank you!"

"You're welcome," Sammy said.

Then Dora turned to face Alejandro. "I don't care about
the gold. I just want to go home with the people I care about."

"Aw, that's so sweet," said Alejandro, mocking the

teenager. "You were going to trade the gold for your parents. Unfortunately, I don't need your help anymore."

Supremely confident in his victory, Alejandro walked into the room, stepping toward the altar. He looked at all the riches assembled, running his fingers along them all. Then he picked up a handful of gold coins.

"The answer is obvious," he said. "The Inca built monuments to their gods with it. Gold is as close to touching the sun as the Inca could get."

"Alejandro, don't!" Dora said, trying to stop the mercenary. "The answer isn't gold!"

"Aw, look. You're trying to trick me. You're angry because I've made a fool of you, but lying doesn't suit you. It's very 'un-Dora,'" Alejandro said.

"I'm not lying!" Dora insisted. "Don't do it!"

"This is chess," Alejandro jeered, "not checkers, my dear. I'm always going to be three steps ahead of you!"

Then Alejandro placed the gold pieces from his hand into the monkey statue's paws. A moment later, the monkey's arms began to rise.

"It's happening!" Alejandro said. "It's happening!"

As the monkey's arms moved upward, the sound of massive, grinding stone gears could be heard, echoing and vibrating throughout the room.

Alejandro anxiously awaited his prize, staring at the monkey statue with avarice.

"You're wrong about me, Alejandro," Dora shouted over the sound of the grinding gears. "I'm not a know-it-all. But

by now, I do know you. I knew you would follow us in here. I knew you would let us take all the risks. I knew the Inca's final test would carry a dire consequence for those who failed it."

The mercenary looked at Dora, a faint glimmer in his eyes that maybe he might have made a mistake.

A colossal, costly mistake.

"I knew you wouldn't listen to me," Dora continued, "and I knew your greed would blind you to the right answer. Which is why we are standing over here. And you . . . you are standing right *there*."

The color drained from Alejandro's face.

"Turns out jungle puzzles are real," Dora said.

Suddenly, the floor that surrounded the altar opened up like a massive trapdoor, and Alejandro fell right inside, into the depths below.

Diego, Sammy, and Randy turned to look at Dora, in awe of their friend. Diego gave her a huge hug.

"I didn't think you had it in you!" he said.

"But how did you know gold was the wrong answer?" Sammy asked.

"Gold was common to the Inca, not something to be revered," Dora said.

"I'm still alive! Help me! Get in here, now!"

Dora looked over toward the trapdoor, and saw that Alejandro was actually still very much alive, hanging on to a tiny outcropping of rock, dangling over the gaping abyss beneath him. In his other hand, he held his walkie-talkie, which he was busy shouting into.

"My mercenaries are on their way!" Alejandro said to Dora. "This isn't over yet!"

Just then, an enormous stone disc in the room rolled aside, revealing a long-hidden passage. There was the sound of footsteps, and shadows thrown on the wall that approached with rapidity.

But the shadows didn't belong to the mercenaries.

They belonged to an old woman, walking down a staircase.

It was the old woman from the opera house ruins. And standing beside her, armed with crossbows, the Lost Guardians of Parapata. The Guardians had the mercenaries with them, captive. And they also had Dora's parents.

"Dora!" shouted Elena and Cole.

"I'm okay!" Dora called out. "We're all okay! I think . . ."

Randy gasped as he looked up. "The Lost Guardians of Parapata . . ." was all he could say.

"Ridiculous!" Alejandro shouted from the pit, unable to see anything. "There are no Lost Guardians! I made them up!"

The old woman stood before them, suddenly arching her back, making herself appear taller. A fog started to gather around her, enshrouding her in mist. As it cleared, the old woman was no longer standing there. In her place was the visage of an empress.

The Inca empress. She was regal and somehow terrifying at the same time. The empress approached the pit with the Guardians, and together, they looked down at Alejandro.

Alejandro gulped.

"Nah, they're super real, bro," Sammy said.

Dora stared into the empress's eyes. "It's her," she said softly.

Then the empress addressed the group in her ancient tongue. "You were warned, and yet you persisted," she said. "We before you are the curse of Parapata. Tasked with keeping the city hidden."

"So is this when we perish?" Sammy asked. "I think this is when we perish."

Not knowing what was about to come next, Randy decided it was now or never. He turned to face Dora and said, "If this is the end, I just want you to now that I love you, Dora, and that this was totally worth it."

"Oh, I love you, too, Randy," Dora said. "I love Diego. And Mami and Papi, and Sammy, and Boots. I love all of you!"

"No, that's not exactly what I meant," Randy tried to explain.

"You have dared to defile Parapata!" said the empress in the old language. "Seize the thieves!"

"No!" Dora said, speaking the empress's language. "We're not with him. We're not treasure hunters. We're explorers. We're here to learn."

The empress looked directly at Dora. It was a serene expression, but severe all the same. "Show me the correct path, explorer," she said.

Then Dora stepped forward to the altar, prepared to make a choice. Both her mother and father started to give her advice but were immediately silenced by the empress. As Dora looked at all the treasures assembled on the altar, she moved past all of them and headed right for the fountain.

"I knew the answer as soon as I saw it," Dora said. "What the Inca revered most was the aqueduct. Drought was their greatest threat. They valued water for their crops and their people."

Then she picked up a bowl, filled it with water from the fountain, and walked over to the monkey statue. Gently, she poured water from the small bowl into the monkey's waiting paws.

The chamber fell silent. Then, the monkey statue raised its hands. Unlike before, panels in the wall began to open on either side of the statue.

The empress looked on, obviously impressed. The faintest hint of a smile played across her lips. "A wise choice," she said in the old language.

The empress then smiled at Dora and motioned for her and her family and friends to come forward. Then they stepped through one of the panels that had opened next to the monkey.

And they couldn't believe what they saw.

"It's more than I . . ." Elena said, her voice trailing off.

". . . ever imagined," Cole said, completing her sentence.

"It's just like you described," Dora said.

"It's breathtaking," Sammy gushed.

"Monkey. Really big gold monkey," was all Randy could say.

Boots was right there next to him, and gave Randy a fist bump. Then suddenly, the temple began to vibrate.

"What's happening?" Sammy shouted.

"Swiper!" Dora yelled.

Sure enough, the frog poison had worn off, and Swiper was once more on his feet. He had scampered into the temple, and was now holding the two-foot-tall monkey statue by its tail, clenched tight in his teeth! It appeared that by grabbing the statue, Swiper had activated another trap . . . and the temple began to collapse in on itself!

"Swiper, no swiping!" Dora called out.

"He has angered the gods," said the empress.

The doorways around Dora and her friends began to cave in, and the chamber walls began to crumble into nothingness.

"Go, go, go!" Cole shouted. "We gotta get out of here!"

"But what about all the gold?" Randy said.

"It doesn't matter!" Elena shouted.

As chaos reigned around them, they noticed that the Lost Guardians had Alejandro in their possession and were dragging him away.

"Wait!" Alejandro screamed. "What about me? You can't leave me here! Dora! We're a team!"

Swiper continued to make good his escape, clutching onto the monkey statue. He raced up a ramp, as Dora and her family and friends went after him. As everything crumbled behind them, Dora cast one last glance into the chamber. She saw the faint outlines of the Lost Guardians, and of the empress, nodding at Dora. The Lost Guardians then grabbed Alejandro and the other mercenaries, dragging them back into the collapsing temple.

"This is all part of my plan!" Alejandro called out, and

then he seemed to disappear, along with the Lost Guardians and the empress.

And right before she turned to escape with her companions, Dora saw the fabled lost treasure.

It would never be seen again.

CHAPTER 26

THEY HAD ESCAPED THE temple,
but the entire city of Parapata was now facing the
devastating collapse that had destroyed the monkey chamber. Everywhere around Dora and her companions, the city
was falling. The ground beneath their feet was shaking as
they ran, in hot pursuit of a small fox with a two-foot-tall
monkey statue.

"Swiper!" Dora yelled. "No swiping! Swiper, no—"

Suddenly, Swiper was at the city gate and had crossed
through. As he did so, the gate itself began to shake.

"I think it's too late, sweetheart," Elena said.

"Come on, we gotta go! I like Parapata, but I don't want
to be stuck here forever!" Cole announced.

They raced through the city gates as they saw Boots suddenly spring up, going after Swiper! The two animals were
now fighting over the monkey statue, with Boots doing his
best to get it away from the wily fox.

"We've got to put the statue back!" Dora said.

Boots tickled Swiper, which caused the fox to laugh like
crazy, and more important, to drop the statue. Then the
monkey scooped up the statue and hurled it toward Dora,
who caught it.

"We're explorers, not treasure hunters," Dora said to
herself. Looking over her shoulder, she took in the city of

Parapata. She saw there was an empty plinth, with two water-falls on either side. It was an exact mirror of what she had seen inside the chamber!

"That's it!" Dora exclaimed. Sprinting back into the crumbling city over the protests of her parents, Dora ran for the plinth. Examining it, she saw there was an indentation about the same size as the base of the monkey statue. Care-fully, she placed the statue into the indentation. There was a loud click, and then all at once, the rumbling stopped.

The city was no longer shaking.

Dora had saved Parapata.

But the enormous gates now began to close!

Taking one last look at the incredible lost city, Dora bolted for the gates. She just managed to slip through as the doors closed, joining her family and friends on the other side.

Dora turned around to watch the gates close completely. Then suddenly, as if by magic, the vines that had covered the gates before started to grow, once more covering the gates.

Forever.

"You are the greatest explorer of all of us," Elena said as she hugged Dora tighter than she ever had before. "Thank you for saving us, Dora. *Te quiero.*"

Cole hugged his daughter as well and said, "*Te quiero.*"

"*Te quiero,*" Dora said.

Then Diego turned to Sammy. "Look, I know we weren't exactly friends when this trip started, but something has changed, and—"

Before he could finish, Sammy grabbed Diego and gave him a kiss.

"I like you, too," she said, and flashed him a warm smile. Then she suddenly had a feeling, like the kind of feeling you get when you think someone's staring right at you. "Dora's staring at us again, isn't she?"

"Yup," said Diego. And sure enough, Dora was watching Diego and Sammy, unable to look away.

Boots coughed, which, while not like a normal monkey thing to do, was a pretty typical Boots thing to do. The monkey motioned toward Swiper, who was trying with all his fox strength to pry open the forever-sealed gates to Parapata.

As one, the group shouted: "Swiper, no swiping! Swiper, no swiping!"

Then Swiper suddenly turned, his face a mask of anger. And . . .

. . . he spoke!

"Stop!" he said. "Stop already! I get it! You all want me to say, 'Aw man!' and scurry off like a good little Swiper. But when does Swiper finally get his?!"

Everyone watched, slack-jawed, as the fox started to pace back and forth. "I had dreams! You think I want to be swiping at my age? Carrying on like a fool in this mask? I'm sixty-five years old, for crying out loud! I live in a studio apartment!"

After a moment, Boots approached Swiper and turned the fox around to face him. The monkey stared at the fox. There was understanding in those eyes.

"You're . . . right," Swiper said. "I am lashing out at them, but really the only person I have to blame . . . is Swiper."

Boots did his staring thing some more.

"Maybe it's not too late for me," Swiper continued. "I can do the work, search my soul, find myself. Find the real Swiper!"

Of course, one thing you should absolutely know—all of Swiper's talking just sounded like fox chatter to Dora and her friends. That's right. They couldn't understand a word of it.

Because ANIMALS CAN'T TALK.

Anyway.

"I can do this!" Swiper said. "No more swiping! No more hiding behind this mask! It's time to show the world who I am!"

Then, with a dramatic flourish, Swiper removed his mask. Underneath, he had white markings on his face in the exact same shape as the mask.

"You have set me free," Swiper said to Boots. "Thank you. You're an incredible listener." Then Swiper grabbed Boots and gave him a hug.

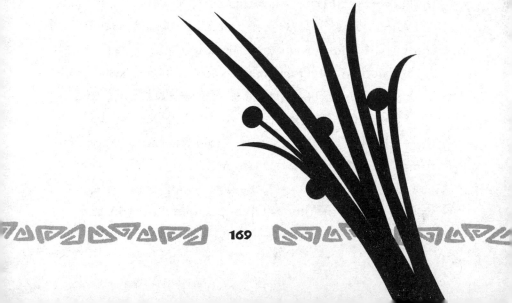

CHAPTER 27

AFTER THEIR EPIC ADVENTURE,
Dora, her friends, and her family first returned to Dora's jungle home. There, the parents and families of Diego, Sammy, and Randy had been waiting. Waiting to give their kids enormous, never-ending hugs, and to take them back home.

Cole and Elena prepared an epic feast for all the families. It would be a night long remembered by everyone involved.

"So, Dora, we have exciting news," Cole announced as they took a break from the dinner.

"We're going into the deep jungle again in a few weeks," Elena said.

"We'll be gone for months. No contact. Just us against the elements. Me. Your mom," Cole said, "and . . . you."

Elena could hardly contain herself. "We're onto something big, even bigger than Ancient Inca—"

"About that," Dora said, interrupting her parents. "I think . . . I think I want to go back to the city."

In that moment, Dora's parents couldn't have been prouder of their daughter. They smiled as Dora held Elena's hand.

"I know the jungle pretty well," Dora continued. "But high school . . . I think I need more time to study the culture . . . and its indigenous people."

Cole and Elena gave Dora another hug, and the teenager walked over to the dinner table and joined her friends.